Cattle Kingdom

ANOTHER SAGEBRUSH LARGE PRINT WESTERN BY
ALAN LEMAY

The Smoky Years

Cattle Kingdom

ALAN LEMAY

Sagebrush
Large Print Westerns

Library of Congress Cataloging-in-Publication Data

LeMay, Alan, 1899-1964.
    Cattle kingdom / Alan LeMay
        p.   cm.
    ISBN 1-57490-285-7 (alk. paper)
    1. Large type books. I. Title

    PS3523.E513 C38 2000
    813'52—dc21   00-040277

Cataloguing in Publication Data is available from
the British Library and the National Library of Australia.

Sagebrush Large Print Westerns are published in the United
States and Canada by Thomas T. Beeler, Publisher, PO Box 659,
Hampton Falls, New Hampshire 03844-0659. ISBN 1-57490-285-7

Published in the United Kingdom, Eire, and the Republic of
South Africa by Isis Publishing Ltd, 7 Centremead, Osney
Mead, Oxford OX2 0ES England. ISBN 0-7531-6258-X

Published in Australia and New Zealand by Bolinda Publishing
Pty Ltd, 17 Mohr Street, Tullamarine, 3043, Victoria, Australia.
ISBN 1-74030-022-X

Manufactured by Sheridan Books in Chelsea, Michigan.

Cattle Kingdom

CHAPTER ONE

"OF COURSE YOU KNEW," THE GIRL SAID, "A MAN HAS been killed, here on the 94 range?"

Billy Wheeler turned to look at the girl who perched beside him on the corral fence, and for a moment he forgot to answer. Marian Dunn hadn't been in the desert country long enough to gather a very heavy tan. Under the shadow of her Stetson her face reflected some of the glow of the fresh morning sunlight upon the red hills; to Billy Wheeler it seemed a fragile face, finely drawn, suggesting transparency. And her eyes were blue distance boiled down. Inescapably she looked like something from some gentler, better country, a magic come from the mysteries beyond the hills. She wore belted overalls and half boots; but she could never have been mistaken for a Westerner.

Billy Wheeler, though, could never be mistaken for anything else. The dry intermountain country, by its necessity of wide ranges and the perpetual mobility of the saddle, has set its mark upon its sons. Wheeler was young, but his weather-trimmed features showed the blast of sun and sweep of wind, and his grey eyes were visibly tuned to distance. He was wearing summer tweeds instead of brush jacket and chaps; yet wherever he might have been, he would still have suggested this land of vast rolling flats, of desert mountains and dry rivers, sage brush and mesquite and gaunt red rock. And afoot or on a fence, he would still always be unmistakably a horseman.

The girl turned her eyes to him, reminding him he was supposed to say something.

1

"I didn't hear much," he said. "A gas station man told me there was a killing, as I came through Inspiration; but he didn't know much about it."

"I guess nobody does."

"Yes, but—who was killed? And when?"

"That's just it," the girl told him. "They don't know who was killed. It's the strangest thing I ever heard of. They can't even find him."

"Can't find who? The man who was killed?"

"That's it."

Billy Wheeler grinned slowly, boyishly. "Well, I'll be darned!"

"I don't think it's funny. I think it's—horrible."

"Well, yes; I guess it is."

He looked away, estimating again the nearness of the approaching riders. John "Red Horse" Dunn, Old Man of the 94, at whose summons Wheeler had come three hundred miles, had not been on hand to receive him, having set out before daylight on an unknown mission with three of his cow hands. But they were coming in now; across the dry morning Wheeler could identify the individual riders at the half mile as they jog-trotted in, their ponies abreast.

"When did all this happen?" he asked.

"Uncle John found the sign, as he calls it, yesterday morning."

"Then he must have wired me right after that."

"I guess so."

She hadn't known, then, that her uncle had sent for him. She hadn't known that he was coming—and he hadn't known she was here. That made a difference.

"Uncle John hasn't wanted to talk about this thing— to me," the girl now said. "Perhaps he'll give you a different, clearer story, Billy."

2

They fell silent. Billy Wheeler let his eyes run over casual, familiar things—the roadster he had come in, the tall barns, the low-sprawled house, bunkhouse, and grub shack. The clapboards of the buildings were warped and cracked, blasted a paintless grey by many a sandy wind. You had to look in the horse corrals, where a big string of grain-fed ponies always loafed, to find signs of efficiency, of means, and of power. But as Billy Wheeler's eyes drifted out over the vast rolling "flats" of the plain, resting here and there on a broken, flat-topped mesa or a far up-thrust mountain of gaunt red rock, all that he saw, excepting only the far peaks, was under the dictatorship of Horse Dunn's brand—the 94.

Billy Wheeler looked at these familiar things, but he was not thinking about them. He was thinking about the girl at his side, whom he hardly looked at at all.

Billy Wheeler had not seen Marian Dunn for two years. Had he known that she was here, he would not have come here now.

Marian Dunn was Horse Dunn's niece. Once, for a couple of months two years ago, Wheeler had seen her every day. He had used every persuasion he knew of, all he had, to make this girl love him—and he had failed. Sometimes he could still hear her low, cool voice: "I'm sorry—truly sorry." The sincere regret in that was pretty hard to take.

In everything else he had succeeded. He had come up from nothing in cows, and tripled in land, and switched back to cows to double again. He had liquidated everything at the peak of cattle prices, and at twenty-seven had nothing to worry about. But in this one thing he cared most about he had met only complete blank defeat. He would not have come here, to raise again the bitterness of that defeat, if he had known that she was here.

And now there was a certain awkwardness between them, since she inevitably knew all that, too.

"I think he's going to ask a favor of you," Marian said.

"I don't know if you know this," Billy Wheeler said slowly; "but his wire made out as if he was offering me a job."

"Yes—I knew that."

"I owe a lot to old Horse Dunn," Billy Wheeler said. "He picked me up when I was fourteen years old, halfway starved and all the way maverick. He carried me along four years. If it wasn't for him, I'd be in the wild bunch—or in the pen. And he showed me my start in cattle.

"I suppose, then," Marian said, "you won't turn him down in this thing now."

"You mean you figure I'll take this job?"

"Why, yes; won't you?"

Billy Wheeler's eyes were fixed dourly on his hands, which were creasing and re-creasing a cigarette paper with meticulous care. He shook his head.

"You've made up your mind, without even talking to him?"

"Yes; just about have."

There was an odd little expression on the girl's quiet face as she asked, "Why, Billy?"

"I've got things to see to, Marian," he stalled. "I couldn't take on another job now."

He supposed she might know that this was not so. For the present he was out from under; he could afford to do anything he wanted to, to fill his time or to help a friend. But to take a job in which he would see this girl every day, while yet tight-cinched by the knowledge that she

4

was not for him, and never would be—that was something else.

"If your uncle wants me to go to San Francisco for him, or Kansas City—might be I could fit that in. But if he aims to work me here at the 94—"

"It's here that he wants you," Marian told him.

They were silent again. Out on the sun-silvered levels the approaching horsemen were at the quarter mile. Behind them a giant plume of dust had risen skyward, showing that the Old Man had now spotted Wheeler's car, and had fanned his riders into a lope.

"I don't know how much he needs you," Marian said; "nor who else he could get, instead. But I know this—he has more enemies than friends, by three to one."

Billy Wheeler stirred restlessly, and began to build a cigarette. He knew it was true that the 94 had many enemies, few friends. Here in this dusty, mesa-broken land Horse Dunn had set out to build a cow kingdom—a kingdom on the grand scale of the old days, when a man could cut out five thousand beeves in the fall work, and five thousand again in the spring, and never miss their number. And before the great slump in cattle prices he had appeared to be near the re-establishment of such a cow kingdom as was hardly known any more, anywhere in the intermountain country.

But you can't build a cow kingdom, buying up the range rights of little brand after little brand, without annoying and disturbing the brands that are left; and the bought-out brands are forever trying to edge back.

Here and there in the world were perhaps half a dozen graves commemorating the drawn-out, inevitable conflict. There had never been a general open war. But more than one lone-riding cowboy of the 94 had come to his end by the gunfire of persons unknown, and one

5

or two others had left on the range an enemy who would force the issue no more. And at Ace Springs had died two men of four—hired gunfighters all—who had jumped Horse Dunn from ambush. The 94 could have started its own Boot Hill.

More effectual than those brief, unofficial bursts of action was the enmity of certain cooler, more wisely watchful men, like Link Bender, Pinto Halliday, Sam Caldwell—the defeated contestants for the Red Hills ranges. Nowadays the expanding 94 found itself encircled by a veritable wolf ring of enemies—a wolf ring biding its time with a malevolent optimism.

"I don't even know what the situation is," the girl went on. "But it's worrying him deeply; he can't hide that, not from me. And his first move was to turn to you."

"Oh, shucks now, Marian . . ."

"I shouldn't like to think," the girl said oddly, as if with difficulty, "that you turned him down because I'm here."

For an instant he sat perfectly still, silent. He hadn't expected her to come out with it, direct and straight like that.

She put both hands on the rail between them and leaned toward him. "I'd never forgive myself if I thought you let Horse Dunn down on account of me. I'll—get out of here, if you want me to."

He looked straight at her—and lied. "Nothing farther from my mind," he assured her. "No call to even think of such a thing."

"It shouldn't be necessary," Marian agreed slowly. "What's in the past is over with and forgotten. Neither one of us ever needs to think of it again."

"Sure," he said; "oh, sure." He paused, listening to

the stampede of hoofs beyond a big barn which obscured the riders as they swung into the layout.

And now rescue came, as Horse Dunn thundered around the corner of the barn and slid his pony to a stop before them in a great up-jump of dust.

CHAPTER TWO

To OLD TIMERS JOHN DUNN WAS KNOWN AS "RED Horse Jack"—or more commonly, just "Horse" Dunn—partly because he was big as a horse, and partly because of the coarse sorrel mane he had had in his youth. Nobody knew how old Horse Dunn was; they thought he must be sixty-eight at least, and his mustache and curly beard were at last roaned with grey. But he seemed to have an Indian medicine on him which cheated time, for he was powerful and barrel-chested yet, straight as a lodgepole pine, and he swung his two hundred pounds in and out of saddles as lightly as a kid bronc rider.

Half an hour after his return Dunn was to be seen leaning against a post of the open gallery which ran along the front of the cook-shack; he was chewing a blade of burro grass. Said he, "We all grant a man is dead. Any of you still doubting that?" He watched the cowboys, who lounged along the open edge of the gallery floor, but none of them answered.

Breakfast had been set out by a little withered old woman known as Tia Cara. She had fed them promptly—and they ate the same way. Horse Dunn was a man who ate enormously, but he set his mind to it, so that his cowboys learned that a meal was a horse race. And Wheeler, sitting at the table between Marian and

7

her uncle, had had no chance to learn why the Old Man of the 94 had sent for him. It had not been long before they were trooping out of the cook shack again.

"Look here," Dunn went on. "Look here! I'm going to ask you once more—and this is the last time. If any of you is a good enough man to have blasted a cow thief, say so now! I'll back any boy of mine that shot in defense of the brand. You know that!"

He paused, and waited. Val Douglas, Dunn's thirty-year-old range boss, let mild eyes dream on a distant peak, and Tulare Callahan spat over his shoulder through his teeth.

"All right," the Old Man said. "I ain't doubting you, any of you. Now I'm telling you what I want you to do. You've seen the killer's trail at Short Crick—the trail of a cup-hoofed pony, long in the toe; been shod, and the shoes pulled off. We've missed out on locating that trail where it left Short Crick. Now I want you to start in and comb this range. Somewhere, somehow, we got to cut that trail. And especially we've got to find the man that's dead."

"Anybody checking back on the dead man's horse?"

"Don't you worry about the dead man's horse. There'll be plenty checking done on that horse! Tulare, you take the flat country to the south. But don't trample any more around Short Crick. Swing wide—five miles wide—and search the brush for a trail hitting toward Warrior Crick, and Santiam."

"Okay."

"Gil, you sweep northwest between Short Crick and the Spotted Range," Dunn went on. "The Spotted Range is full of horse bands, and the ground is baked cruel hard; but try it, anyway. Val, you take a wider swing than Gil, and to the east. Scout the edge of the bare rock

8

below Red Sleep Ridge. If the killer somehow got up on that rock, God knows where he come off it."

"Ain't Red Sleep a little far?"

"We better hope so. But you go look."

The cowboys waited. "Is there any guess yet," Tulare asked after a moment, "as to *who it is* we're looking for?"

Unexpectedly the Old Man flared up. "How the hell do I know!" he roared. "And what do *you* care? You'll know him when you find him because he's dead! Ain't that enough for you? What you waiting for now? Get on with it!"

They moved off, and were presently to be seen straggling out of the layout with a deceptive appearance of leisure, their ponies at the running walk or jog. Men who must travel a long way do not jump their horses into a run.

Horse Dunn turned to Billy Wheeler. "Get your war bag. You got to get into horse pants and boots. You and I got some riding of our own to do, no later than now!"

Billy Wheeler jerked suitcase and saddle from his roadster and followed Horse Dunn to a room in the rambling weathered house—the only room the Old Man used when he was alone. There wasn't much in it except a springless bunk with clean folded blankets on it, some fine old saddles on racks fixed to the wall, and various guns hung on hooks and pegs. The puncheon floor, polished almost white by innumerable sandy sweepings, was very clean.

Here, while Wheeler changed to cow-country work clothes, Horse Dunn stood looking out across the range. Presently he took the white silk handkerchief from his neck, shook it out, and refolded it. Dunn was hardly ever seen without that clean white handkerchief, fresh

9

every day. He wound it flat around his neck like a stock, and drew the ends through a black cow-horn ring under one ear. And when this was done he turned to Billy Wheeler, his big crinkly-bearded face unreadable.

"Look out the window. Look over at Lost Whiskey Buttes. You see a signal there?"

Wheeler obeyed. Four miles off, on a high place, he made out a thin vertical line against the brassy sky.

"That's Steve Hurley's smoke," Horse Dunn told him. "Last night Steve was in Inspiration, checking up. This morning—he's been on that butte since before daybreak."

"What's the smoke mean, Horse?"

"It means the sheriff is on the ride—he's left Link Bender's, headed for Short Crick. Maybe you think he's getting a slow start. He is. That's the nature of the man. You ready?"

"Lead out," said Wheeler, buckling his chap belt.

"Wait."

Horse Dunn reached down a broad cartridge belt whose holster carried a heavy six-gun, and swung this about his waist. "Pick yourself a gun," he told Wheeler.

"What's this for?" Wheeler demanded.

"In case of emergency, boy."

Wheeler hesitated. Like many a western youngster, he had played with guns all his life. But because he was young his memory did not go back to the times when a man's gun was the whole of the law; he had never carried a gun either as a defense or as a threat. He felt like a fool, arming himself as if he were some wild-eyed kid looking for trouble and likely to find it. "I don't need any gun, Horse," he said.

"I don't believe you'll find it makes you look unstylish," Horse Dunn told him slowly. "Styles in gents' apparel has changed a little around here, since you worked this range. And maybe we'll find they've changed still more—just since yesterday. Never mind it, though, if it makes you uneasy."

Wheeler stared at him a moment more. Then he shrugged, picked a weighted gunbelt from the wall, and strapped it on.

"Bring your saddle."

At the corrals Horse Dunn pointed out a stocky buckskin pony, and when Billy Wheeler had roped and rigged this animal, Dunn led the way out of the layout. Promptly Horse Dunn pushed his own tall sorrel into a hard lamming trot.

"I want to join up with the sheriff somewheres about Chuck Box Wash," Dunn explained. "I'm right anxious to be with him when he makes his look-see at Short Crick."

"Horse," said Billy Wheeler, "what's happened here?"

"You'll see for yourself, better than I can tell you, knowing the lay of country like you do. But I'll tell you what I know."

In abrupt sentences he told Wheeler what had happened.

Morning of the day before, Horse Dunn had been riding Short Creek in the course of making a cattle count. The range of the 94 was far-flung and broken; the first step toward a count was to read the water holes, to find out what part of the range the big bunches were frequenting. Reading sign on Short Creek, Dunn had come upon the double trail of a shod horse and an unshod horse, ridden side by side. The trail was going his way. He rode along it without attention—until he came upon blood-stained ground.

11

"I studied the ground very careful, tracing the trails," Dunn said. "In five minutes I knew for sure I'd come on the place where a man met his death."

"But there was no body?"

Dunn shook his head. "The dead man keeled out of the saddle as he was shot," he reported the sign. "But I guess he got stirrup hung, for he was dragged. His pony pulled him through the crick. I followed across, and found where he come loose. But the dead man was no more there."

"I don't know as I get this," Wheeler said.

Dunn gave it as his opinion that the man on the other horse had followed and picked up his victim. "When I saw that," said Dunn, "I knew I was looking at the beginning of something. Maybe—at the beginning of the end."

Wheeler, sitting his pony with a deft and compact balance, stared at the huge old man. Horse Dunn spoke without description, almost without expression; but Wheeler, knowing the range, could see the Old Man of the 94 beside the sun-blasted cuts of Short Creek, sitting detached upon a pony that snorted and shied from those darkened stains. And he could see a double trail, faint on the baked dusty earth—a dim, half-understood trail, that somehow seemed leading into unknown misfortune.

For a moment Wheeler stared at Dunn; then the spell broke. The continued assumption that a man had been killed, though no dead man had been found, was getting to be too much for Wheeler. Men who spent their lives in those vast intermountain ranges knew how to read trail as a city man reads print, and Dunn was as good as most. But to assume flatly that a man was killed, when even the identity of the victim was unknown, seemed to Wheeler an outlandish stretch, even for an old tracker.

12

"This is the darndest thing I ever heard of, Horse," Wheeler complained. "What—no corpse? What the hell kind of murder is this? Who's missing?"

"Nobody's missing, that's known yet."

"Well, what I don't see," Wheeler said, "is why you were in such a hurry to report to the sheriff, with so little known."

"I had no choice. I was still looking over the ground when I sighted a rider, about a mile off. In a minute I made out it was Link Bender. Maybe you can remember when Link's Seven S was bigger than the 94. Maybe you remember how he tried to pinch out the 94—almost put Marian's father to the wall. I broke him of all that! But he's never swallered that he was licked. I've got plenty enemies, Billy; but Link Bender is the smartest of 'em. Naturally I couldn't leave it so's he could report he seen me sneaking away. So I had to signal him over and show him what I found."

"And he read the sign the same as you?"

"Billy, I keep telling you! There ain't any other way to read that sign."

"Yes, but look here—the supposed dead man's horse—"

"Link Bender took off on the trail of the dead man's horse. Hoping to find the body, like a fool. I let him go, and haven't seen him since. So I don't know what he found. But he went and reported to the sheriff, like I knew he would."

"I should think you'd have been some interested in the dead man's *caballo* yourself.

"More interested in the other side of it. The killer's trail took to the crick. Short Crick runs two hands deep on stone for two miles, then disappears in the sand. I took to the crick and hunted for where the killer left it.

13

Plenty horse bands water at Short Crick, wading in and out. I lost the trail.

"So pretty soon," Horse Dunn finished, "I rode back to the ranch. By that time it had come to me what I might be up against here. So I had a wire sent to you."

They trotted two miles in silence. "I've been trying to figure out," Billy Wheeler said at last, "where I fit in this."

Dunn was silent for a little way. "I've got enemies, Billy," he said finally.

"A few head of 'em," Wheeler agreed.

"Before heaven," Dunn said, "I've give every man his just dues! But plenty people think I've pushed on the reins, trying to make the 94 a great brand. Rufe Deane blames me for the death of his son—which God knows I had no hand in. Pinto Halliday swears I cut the ground from under him through the shark loan companies. Link Bender claims I swamped a range—over-grazed and wrecked it—to put him down. Lies, all lies!"

This Billy Wheeler understood. "I know."

"And you know, too," Dunn reminded him, "the cow country is in terrible bad shape. Everybady has had to borrow, for three years straight. Nobody has borrowed deeper than the 94. Now our debts come due again. I have to go to Las Vegas, maybe to San Francisco. It's a close call, by God, to keep the 94 out of bankruptcy! Now suppose this coyote ring, with Link Bender at the head of it, can force some trouble onto the 94. Suppose that trouble is made to look bad enough so that I can't extend those loans—let alone increase 'em? The work of fifteen years drops from under like a shot pony!"

Wheeler frowned. "There used to be a pretty square bunch running the county offices at Inspiration," he said.

14

"There was while Tom Amos was alive. He's dead; his boy is sheriff—and he isn't man enough for it. Link Bender's ring runs the whole show. They're fixed to make a case stick, all right—for a little while—even if it's a poor one. And boy, we don't know yet if the case is going to be poor."

"I can't see yet where they have any case at all," Wheeler said flatly.

"The killing is on my range. Easy to get holt of a motive."

Wheeler considered. "But when the body is found—"

"Who knows what'll be found?—if Link Bender's people are the ones to find it! Maybe that the dead man couldn't possibly be a cow thief. Maybe he was shot in the back, muzzle to his shirt. Maybe he was unarmed."

"And maybe somebody shot a jack rabbit," Wheeler suggested.

"Who ever seen a jack rabbit on a horse?" Dunn shrugged. "It's going to be almighty necessary that we know more about this than the other fellers, Billy. I sent for a good man to help us with that end of it. I sent for Old Man Coffee of McTarnahan."

"I've heard of him. I guess he's pretty good on a trail. But still I don't see where I fit, Horse."

"Suppose Link Bender's crowd can work it out to hold me on some trumped-up charge—sixty, ninety days? Long enough for the 94 to go to pieces in the face of its called loans? There's going to be more to pulling the 94 through the landslide than a wagon boss like Val Douglas can handle. There's got to be a different man on the ground—and that man is you."

For a moment Wheeler was deeply troubled. If, by any chance, Horse Dunn's prophesies should prove correct, Wheeler did not see how he could refuse the old

15

man the assistance he asked. But evidently this would mean that Wheeler would have to sign on to help with the management of the 94.

Thinking of this awkward possibility, he thought again of the blue eyes of Marian Dunn, of the strangely lovely glow of her face in the reflected light of the red-gold hills. For him there was a magic in that girl. It was a magic which could humble a man, and break him, heart and soul; taking the light out of every victory he might win, when only she turned away her face. And he heard her voice, full of that same magic still: "I'm sorry—truly sorry . . ."

It was his hope to forget this girl, to learn to build his life around other things. And he knew that he would never be able to forget her while he lived, if now again he should have to live near her, seeing her every day of the world—unable to shut her face away even by darkness, or by closing his eyes. He could not refuse Horse Dunn—yet, under the circumstances, neither could he come to Dunn's aid. If Dunn was right—

Wheeler came to himself, and shrugged it off. The old man's wary movements of defense before any blow was struck showed Wheeler how much store the Old Man of the 94 set upon the security and the future of his brand, so that suddenly he felt sorry for Horse Dunn. To mind came a fragment of song that seemed to him singularly appropriate to Horse Dunn's case; and he hummed it under his breath.

"I had a hoss named Baldy,
        He was a pain to me,
For spooks kept after Baldy—
        They wouldn't leave him be.
"And every time he seen a spook,
        You should of heard him yell;

16

He loosed all holts and come unwound,
And bucked me flat as hell."
"What's that song?" Horse demanded suspiciously.

"It's an Indian song, called 'Bury Me Upside Down,' " Wheeler lied.

"Wait," Dunn said, as if he had read Wheeler's mind. "Wait and see."

Far ahead dark specks of horsemen showed, emerging from Chuck Box Wash as if from the surface of the plain. Dunn booted his pony into a lope.

CHAPTER THREE

WALT AMOS, SHERIFF OF THE RED HILLS COUNTRY, was a youngish man, with a direct but mild grey-green eye; though he carried no excess weight he had those rounded features which make the faces of certain men appear as cornerless and unobjectionable as an egg. He led a low-headed pony by a rope to his saddle horn.

"I'm right glad you rode over, Horse," he said when the 94 men had drawn up. "You'll be able to help Link, here, recall how the sign looked when you first seen it."

Behind him, lounging in their saddles, sat three others. These, Wheeler knew, were Link Bender, tall, hawk-faced, close-lipped; Link's son, a lanky, weasel-faced youth whom Wheeler knew only as "the Kid"; and Cayuse Cayetano, a saffron-faced Indian breed who wore a circular shield marked "Indian Police" upon a green and black checked shirt.

These three had nodded in greeting, but said nothing; and now there was a moment's awkward pause. In the silence could be heard an irregular moaning sound somewhere far to the north—the bellowing of cattle

17

working themselves into a state of mind over some unknown thing.

"I was figuring to ride over to your place later, anyway, Dunn," the sheriff said. "I was especially kind of hoping you'd recognize this horse."

"Link Bender—" Dunn said slowly—"he found him, did he?"

"He found the horse—this horse; not the man."

Dunn studied the led horse at the sheriff's flank. "So this," Dunn said, "is the horse a feller got killed on."

The horse the sheriff led was a runty bay of the wild pony type which infests the intermountain ranges from border to border. It bore no brand; but broad on the withers and extending downward on the off side almost to the knee were the dust-crusted stains of yesterday's blood.

Dunn leaned low to study the feet of the led horse. "It's the horse from Short Crick, all right," he said at last. "No, I never seen him before."

The sheriff looked hopefully at Wheeler, but Billy Wheeler shook his head.

"Nobody knows the damn animal!" the sheriff burst out fretfully. "I'd have thought you fellers would know every horse in the country by this time."

"You get around as much as anybody," Dunn grunted. He studied the pony's hackamore—a common rope hackamore such as might have been any man's. "Where's the saddle?"

"Link didn't find any saddle."

Dunn glanced at the dark, lean-visaged Link Bender. "Dead man must have taken his saddle with him across the big divide," he commented sarcastically.

Sheriff Amos looked irritated. "Well, come on; we'll look over the ground."

18

They turned and rode northward at a jog. A curious tension had come over them for no plain reason. It showed in the bony, tight-drawn features of Link Bender; his face was as expressionless as rock, except that his mouth, half hidden by his mustache, was a hard clamped line. It showed too in Kid Bender's face, in the form of a kind of hard, sarcastic-looking wariness; and in the shifty-eyed detachment of Cayuse Cayetano, who seemed to wish his connection with the sheriff's party to be as little noticed as possible. As for the sheriff himself, he was irritable and restless—a man too much worried by too little.

They were nearing Short Creek; and the bellowing of cattle had become near and strong—a fantastic deep booming broken by whistling soprano squalls. "What the devil them steers raising hell about?" Amos demanded querulously.

Nobody answered him. They rode in a peculiarly oppressive silence, a silence somehow unnatural and ominous, even among these naturally quiet men. Now as they rounded the shoulder of Two Bull Butte they sighted the disturbed cattle at the quarter mile, a dark milling knot, restless with tossing horns.

Link Bender raised his clenched hands to the sky and swore abruptly, savagely. "There goes your sign! There goes your evidence, and your trails!"

Billy Wheeler's scalp crawled; men might misread the sign, but the cattle knew. One of the strangest things of the range, and the source of many a weird legend, was the way the big white-faced range steers would come for miles to mark the place of a killing, bawling and pawing, and throwing the dirt over their backs.

The sheriff said in a strange voice, "Is that the place?"

"Sure it's the place! The fool critters have swarmed in

19

on the smell of blood!"

Wheeler heard Horse Dunn curse between his teeth. The Old Man jumped his pony forward, whipping up side and side, and charged down upon the milling cattle. The others joined him, whooping and whipping up their ponies.

The steer bunch broke reluctantly, half inclined to face out the charging riders. Link Bender seized the tail of a steer, hooked it over his saddle horn, and threw the animal into a somersault with the rush of his horse; then tailed and threw a second and a third. One of them, getting up with a horn broken off, rushed bucking through the other cattle, stirring them into movement. After that the herd got under way, and moved off; but even then some of the cattle turned at a distance to stand watching in a ragged semicircle, bawling and pawing still.

Wheeler had been less interested in the running off of the cattle than in the reactions of the riders. All signs would have been obliterated; he was anxious now to see who would be exasperated and who indifferent. Watching, he noted the conspicuous fury of Link Bender, the red-eyed anger of Horse Dunn—and the watchful detachment of Cayuse, the Indian.

The riders were gathering again, disgruntled as they focused upon the stretch of creek the cattle had trampled. Horse Dunn brought his pony near to that of Link Bender.

"You make almighty free with 94 cattle," he said. "Who told you to tail over them steers?"

"Might be," Bender answered, meeting his eye, "you was just as well pleased to see them steers blot out the sign, huh?"

Sheriff Walt Amos drifted his horse between them.

20

"Cut it out," he snapped. "I don't want any of that—you hear? Whether there's any sign left or not, you two know what you saw. I want that dope now—inch by inch."

Dunn shrugged. "Keep back a little, all of you," he said. "I'll show you just what I first found here."

He circled a little and brought them to Short Creek again two hundred yards up-stream.

"Here you see my trail as I come up to the crick," he said; "it's the trail of the same horse I'm riding today . . . Here you see the trail of the two horses of the killer and the feller that was killed, riding side by side along the rim of the cut. Right here my trail comes on to theirs. You, Amos—notice that my trail is twenty hours younger'n the other two."

"I'm not so sure," Link Bender said.

The sheriff hesitated, studying the tracks glumly from the saddle. He turned to the Indian. "What do you say, Cayuse?"

Cayuse Cayetano spoke briefly and promptly in Spanish. "This horse of Dunn's came yesterday," he said. "The other two horses, maybe one day before. Not the same time."

"That Indian's a deer hunter," Sheriff Amos said. "When Cayuse says he knows, he knows. We'll let it stand at that."

"You'll have to take my word for it from here on," Dunn told them. "The cattle sure smeared it up. But anyway—here the two-horse trail dropped down into the crick bed. So did I."

He led them down into the cut and along the margin of the water. Only cattle tramplings showed in the little rifts of sand on stone.

Dunn moved a hundred yards down stream, checked

21

his landmarks, and stopped. "Here's where the feller was shot," he said; "he keeled out of the saddle. His horse stampeded across the crick, running some sideways. The feller was being dragged, like from the stirrup."

Dunn turned and led across the shallow water. "As I rode up this bank," he told the sheriff, "I seen that the trail of the killer was following the trail of the stampeded horse—the same as I." He led on another fifty yards across a maze of cattle tramplings. "Here," he said finally, "is where the feller broke loose from the saddle."

"How'd you know he fell loose here?" Amos asked.

"Because he wasn't dragged no further," Dunn said shortly.

For a moment now they sat staring morosely at a shallow bowl-like pit which the dusty pawing of the cattle had dug. In that silence the bawling of the steers moved closer again. There was something horrible about the stubborn fascination of the cattle, as if something resistless and unseen had sent the uncomprehending brutes here to dig a shallow grave.

"This what you saw, Link?" Sheriff Amos asked.

Bender nodded. "So far."

"The trail of the killer turned back from here," Dunn said. "It took to the crick. I tried to find where it come out of the crick. There was too many horse tracks from the range stock; I never found where it come out. While I was trying to trail it, Link Bender come by and I hailed him. After I showed him what I found he took off after the dead man's horse."

There was a long pause. "This all you fellers got to show?" the sheriff said at last.

"That's all," Dunn said.

22

Link Bender nodded. "I lost the trail of the dead feller's horse," he said shortly. "I swung wide and found the horse further on, but I never seen the saddle."

The sheriff sat his horse for almost a full minute, as if in thought. He seemed about to speak, then apparently thought better of it. Silently he led back the way they had come. They were nearly back to Chuck Box Wash before anyone spoke.

"This is a pretty bad thing, Dunn," Amos said tentatively at last. "The big end of the Red Hills cowmen are pretty well stirred up."

"Funny," Dunn said dryly, "how quick the word got round."

They had come to the forking of their trails, where Dunn would turn westward toward his home ranch. They pulled up their horses.

"Dunn," the sheriff said, "you wasn't figuring to go any place, was you?"

"Amos," said Horse Dunn, "what you mean by that?"

The sheriff met his eye directly, but without pleasure. "I'll have to ask you not to leave the county, Dunn."

Horse Dunn was visibly angering. "Name your reason, then!"

"We haven't any *corpus delicti* yet," the sheriff admitted. "But you grant there's been a killing. This killing is on your range. Of course, first thing everybody thinks is that some one of the 94 outfit shot him a cow thief; but—"

"I'll tell you this," Dunn said. "If I'd had a chance to down a cow thief, I'd have downed him, all right. And I'd have brought him in to you, across his own saddle!"

"That's just it, Dunn," the sheriff pointed out. "Nobody brought him in. He isn't even found. If somebody is trying to hide this thing, then it ain't any

23

common cow-thief killing; it's murder, is what it is. There's something almighty funny going on here, Dunn."

Suddenly Billy Wheeler remembered that Dunn was facing out something greater than two or three men on horses. Link Bender stood for a whole ring of half-whipped brands—the wolf ring, waiting hopefully on its haunches; Sheriff Amos represented a county. Behind these men were numbers and strength—and against the many the Old Man of the 94 stood opposed as a powerful thumb opposes the fingers of a hand.

"And so," Horse Dunn thundered, "you take it on yourself to tell me where I'll go and come!"

"There's plenty stuff has to be cleared up," the sheriff said stubbornly. "One thing, why was those two unknown fellers riding toward the home ranch of the 94?"

"How do I know that?" Dunn demanded. "If they're like the average run of the Red Hills, they was most likely looking for something to steal!"

"All the more reason we have to know where you are," the sheriff retorted. "If it's a cow thief that's dead, who would shoot him on your range but you or one of your boys?"

"Not one of my neighbors." Horse Dunn let his eyes drift to Link Bender's face. "No, not them! They'd never make a move—unless it was to hand the feller his brander."

Instantly Link Bender said, "What do you mean by that?"

In the little moment before Horse Dunn's reply, Billy Wheeler glanced about him, noting the position of the men. Of them all, only Cayuse Cayetano appeared to be unarmed. Link Bender sat alongside the sheriff, but

24

separated from him by the led horse. Wheeler saw him exchange a quick glance with his son, who sat detached, a little to one side. With one spur Wheeler woke his pony, so that it moved sideways, nearer Kid Bender. No one noticed; their eyes were expressionless but intent upon Horse Dunn.

Dunn had swung slowly in his saddle to face Link Bender. "My calf crop is short, is what I mean."

Watching Kid Bender, Wheeler did not see Link make his play; but as Kid Bender's hand dropped to his holster, Wheeler knew that the Kid had taken his cue from Link, who in that instant must have gone for his gun. In the shock of action Wheeler forgot his own weapon, which he had never drawn on any man. He jumped his horse at Kid Bender, striking down on the Kid's gun hand with his quirt. The quirt whistled and bit; as he jerked it back Wheeler felt the gun come with it, tangled in the snap of the lash.

In the same instant a gun roared behind him, and he whirled his pony.

Horse Dunn held the smoking muzzle of his gun skyward and steadied his half-stampeded horse with his other hand. In his face was such a white blaze of fury as Wheeler had never seen. He was not roaring now; his words came through his teeth, hard-edged as broken rock. "I could have killed you," he said, almost as if he were strangling. "And I'd have done it, if only—"

Link Bender sat straight up, his face the dusty grey-green of the brush. Evidently he rode a gun-proof horse, for the reins hung slack on its neck, but it stood. Bender's left hand gripped his right arm; he swayed slightly, but recovered himself, and the color slowly began to come back into his face.

Sheriff Amos brought his hand empty away from the

25

gun-butt to which it had dropped, and let both hands be seen in plain sight upon his reins. His face was discolored by a red flush. "You all right, Link?"

Link Bender said between set teeth, "Good enough."

"You go on home," Walt Amos said to Dunn. "I can't take you in for this because I can't prove you were first to draw. But—"

Dunn said, "You know damn well who was first to draw!"

"Maybe I do and maybe I don't," the sheriff said. "But let me tell you this, Dunn: you've just about run out your rope! By God, if ever a man overplayed his hand, you've sure overplayed yours! You go on home, and see that you stay where you can be got, until you hear from me!"

Horse Dunn grinned, showing his teeth. "I *am* home," he answered. "You fellers are the visitors here. Set off easterly, and ride steady, and maybe in three-four hours you'll be off my range! I'd start at it, if I was you."

He moved off a little way into the scant shade of a Joshua stalk; then sat where he was. Presently, still sitting there, he watched them ride away, losing shape in the heat waves and the dust.

CHAPTER FOUR

OLD MAN COFFEE SURPRISED THEM ALL BY COMING IN on a mule an hour after breakfast next morning. The Frying Pan Country from which he came was beyond the all but inaccessible Tuscaroras, and to reach the 94 by road or narrow-gauge would have called for nearly eight hundred miles of travel. Coffee, however, had apparently come by unsuspected short cuts; and he had

26

come fast and hard, to judge by the ribby and droop-lipped condition of his black mule.

Marian Dunn had never seen an outfit like that of Old Man Coffee. Around the black mule as it shuffled to a stop, no less than six flop-eared dogs of a fox-hound type dropped to the ground. One of these, a big spotted hound with enormous jowls, wore a pack which seemed to contain a tightly-rolled blanket, a frying pan, and a coffee can with a haywire bale. Another, a grizzled ancient hound, astounded Marian because it was wearing deer-skin rock-moccasins, which looked to the girl as if the dog wore shoes—and socks.

The mule's saddle bore a high-power rifle, a pair of hobbles, a cowbell stuffed with leaves, and Old Man Coffee. The old lion hunter's face was of deep-seamed leather, from which deep-set eyes looked out penetratingly, but not unkindly. His faded blue work clothes were like those of the cow hands, but he wore flat-heeled shoes instead of half boots, and instead of the broad Stetson of the cowboys, the mountain man wore slantwise on his bald head a battered hat of a narrow-brimmed, indiscriminate character.

"Don't you find riding a mule kind of slow?" Marian ventured.

Coffee exchanged a brief glance with Horse Dunn. "Oh, sure," he said; "but what's time to a mule?"

"A mule makes mighty good time in the hills, with a good mountain man on him," Horse explained to his niece. "Take now. He's come anyway a hundred and fifty, sixty miles since day before yesterday noon. And what way he took through the Tuscaroras, God only knows. I wasn't looking for him for maybe a week yet. See?"

Marian glanced at her big old uncle but didn't

answer. To the best of Wheeler's knowledge she hadn't spoken to Horse Dunn that morning. Something had come between Horse Dunn and his niece, just since the day before. Horse had a baffled, apologetic look whenever he looked at her. It was wonderful how gentled and saddle-broke the tough Old Man seemed in the case of anything this slim, pale girl was mixed into.

"You'll be wanting some grub and a bunk, Coffee," Dunn assumed. "Tia!" he bellowed at the cook shack. "Set out some—"

"Forget it," said Old Man Coffee shortly. "When I'm hungry I shoot something and eat it. And what in all hell would I want with a bunk? Think I rode two nights and ganted a mule looking for a place to sleep? Just leave your cook skid some meat down these hounds, and I'll call it square."

Old Man Coffee, Horse Dunn, and Billy Wheeler sat in Horse Dunn's room and talked it over. Horse had invited Marian into the conference, but her mysterious aloofness toward her uncle continued, and she had not come. Most of the cowboys were already an hour gone, going on with their patient searching of the brush for the trail of the killer's horse.

"Well," Old Man Coffee came to the point, "who shot who this time?"

Briefly, Horse Dunn explained to Old Man Coffee the curious circumstance by which they knew, or supposed they did, that a man was dead by violence—while still they did not know who he was. He described in some detail the ground marks which the cattle had now erased.

Coffee nodded. Billy Wheeler noted that Coffee, the man of dim trails which only dogs could find, did not question Horse Dunn's interpretation of the sign.

Possibly to Old Man Coffee a set of trails which could actually be seen seemed such simple reading that it did not occur to him that anyone of sense could mistake their meaning.

"And since when," Coffee inquired, "do you get so stirred up over a possible cow-thief shot?"

"It isn't that," Dunn told him. Horse Dunn now tried to explain to Old Man Coffee why Link Bender's coyote ring could be counted on to make the most out of a mystery killing as a weapon against the 94; but Coffee interrupted him.

"I'll take your word for all that claptrap, Horse. You always was a great hand to bite off more than you could swaller."

"They showed their teeth a little bit already," Horse Dunn said, "just in a small way. Walt Amos has reared up and showed his sheriff authority; he ordered me to hold to the county. It made me so whooping mad I turned on Link Bender and put a name to him to his face; he drew on me—I had to shoot him loose from his gun. By God, if it hadn't been for the funny way Marian looks at such things I'd have killed him where he sat! But I only shot him through the arm."

"Worst thing you could have done," Coffee commented.

"He had it coming to him," Horse Dunn said stubbornly.

"Ever get a flesh wound in the arm?" Coffee asked. "I'll tell you about a flesh wound in the arm. Amounts to just enough so you can't sleep, so you lie awake and you think about the feller that give it to you. Night after night, alone in the dark, with a hammer pounding in your arm to keep you at your work. If Link's crowd doesn't swarm all over you it won't be his fault."

29

"He'll come on, all right," Horse Dunn said.

"You figure Link aims to fog you into the calaboose?" Old Man Coffee almost smiled. "By God, I wouldn't have missed it! You'll sure be a sight looking out through the bars of that little jug at Inspiration. I can hear you holler already—voice just slightly muffled by whiskers—'Leave me out and I'll whip every son-of-a—' "

Horse Dunn stared at him sourly.

"I take it, all you want me to find out," said Old Man Coffee, "is what happened to who, what for, and who done it. That cover it?"

"And where is the killer now," Dunn added.

Old Man Coffee locked bony fingers behind his bald head, and sat staring out the window. Beyond the dusty screen spread the barren Red Hills Country, vast and broken; a gaunt, motionless, silent country, red and brassy in the blaze of its sun. There was sullen blue and smoky purple in its distances, and dead white in its alkali sinks; but mostly that country was like blood-tarnished brass—red by the long up-thrust slopes of its Red Hills rock, brassy by the blast of the sun upon its plains.

Old Man Coffee, however, was probably not looking at the color. "Who's been over the ground?" he suddenly demanded.

"Walt Amos, the sheriff. Link Bender. His boy, they call the Kid. My cowboys here—though I didn't let them trample the sign. An Indian deer hunter by the name of Cayuse Cayetano."

Coffee pricked up his ears at the last name. "Cayetano," he repeated. "How long has this Cayetano been over here?"

"About two years, going on three. Had relatives

30

among the Pintwater Piutes; they took him in."

"Broad, flat face, with one eyelid drooped a little from where he was once stung by a bee?"

"That's the one."

"He used to be over in the Frying Pan Country," Old Man Coffee said. "What a sweet character *he* is! Got run out of the Frying Pan by common consent. That was about a year after he beat up the Chinese girl. He—"

"Can he track?"

"He couldn't track a barrel of tar through a—" Coffee stopped. He looked angry and disgruntled. "No," he corrected himself, "that ain't so. He's a good tracker. He's better than that—he's a great tracker. Maybe the best I've ever seen. What a fine turn of the ace this is for me—just as I was figuring I could go on home!"

"Go home? You just got here!"

"And I was just fixing to turn around and go back!" Coffee said. "What's there here for me? Forty million damn fools have blundered all over the ground. Not satisfied with that, you let a big herd of cattle paw it all up. You done everything possible to turn this thing into something that would just drag along until somebody squealed on somebody. What's there in that to keep a man from his work? But now you go to work and run in this Cayuse Cayetano!"

"What's Cayetano got to do with it?"

"He's got everything to do with it," Old Man Coffee snapped. "Cayetano has just enough white blood to make him cussed mean. He's sneaking and he's treacherous, and he hasn't enough guts to lift a sleeping hen off a roost for fear she'd kick him—unless he could club her down from behind. But he can track a cactus wren through a cholla thicket, and if he's left alone on this case he'll make fools of you all."

31

"He's pretty good, is he?"

"I think he can smell a cold trail like a hound," Coffee said grouchily, "and make a fool of the hound. Or maybe he just guesses. But I can tell you this—Cayuse Cayetano will go through this case a-whistling."

"What's the answer then?"

"Oh, I suppose I'll have to go out and take a look, and mess around, and make a fool of myself," Old Man Coffee growled. "First thing, I'll go out and get you the dead man's saddle. I'll get it all right—if Cayetano hasn't got it already. After that I'll find out where the killer's horse come out of the crick. That ought to be enough for one day; when I've done that I'll come home to supper."

"When you going? Now?"

"Sure I'm going now. When did you suppose?"

"We'll go with you as soon as you're ready to start. I—"

"The hell you will," said Coffee. "I only got one dog that won't call me a fool if I tell him to trail a horse. That's old Rock, and he's funny. If he thinks people is watching him he flourishes around trying to look smart, and don't get anything done. Give me one cowboy that's seen the ground—one that'll come home when I send him. And you stay here."

"Oh, well," Horse Dunn grumbled, "suit yourself. I'm only the victim in this case."

"Well, give me a horse, give me a horse—we going to sit here all day?"

For once Horse Dunn did as he was told. Glumly he watched Old Man Coffee go jogging out of the layout, the black hound dogging it at the pony's heels.

CHAPTER FIVE

WILL HE FIND THE SADDLE?" WHEELER ASKED.

"I suppose so," said Horse Dunn gloomily. "But damnation! Much as it means to me, I pretty near hope he won't. The cocky old snort!"

He turned and walked off, and Wheeler followed as Dunn wandered aimlessly through his layout, getting a piece of jerky to chew out of the cook shack, climbing a corral fence to sit morosely staring at the stock—then immediately climbing down again. He ended where he had started—in the house.

"I guess I'll saddle a pony and take a look around here myself," Wheeler said.

"Wait a minute," Horse Dunn said. "There's something different I want you to do."

Billy Wheeler waited, but Horse Dunn seemed to hesitate. "I wish," he said at last, slowly, "I wish you'd talk to that girl."

Wheeler was startled. "Talk to her? About what, Horse?"

"Well, I'll tell you." Horse Dunn groped. "It's this way." He hesitated; out among the barns could be heard the grief-stricken hullabaloo of the hounds Coffee had left behind.

"You two had some kind of a fall-out, didn't you?" Wheeler asked.

"You might call it that," Horse Dunn shrugged. "She doesn't understand the way you have to handle things on this range. And now she's down on me for blasting Link Bender free of his gun."

Billy Wheeler said, "I don't see how she can throw

33

that up to you. Link drew first."

Horse Dunn sat humped at his table, propping himself on his folded arms; and Wheeler noticed again how the fire went out of this tempestuous old man whenever his niece came into the picture.

"She doesn't understand," Horse Dunn repeated. "She's just a kid, Billy; and her mother raised her in the east, in a little town with houses all set close together on a little paved street. And if your neighbor's dog barks at you, you call a constable or somebody, and you say, 'Abate that nuisance.' Then pretty quick the nuisance is abated. How could she understand this here?"

Wheeler admitted there was not much chance. Marian Dunn had been born in this house in which they now sat; she was the daughter of Horse Dunn's brother who had once run the 94. But her father had died when Marian was five years old, and, so far as Wheeler knew, Marian Dunn had since visited the 94 but once in her life—two years ago, when she was eighteen.

"Why, she can't hardly even believe that this country is here," Dunn continued. "They've taught her that the country is all settled up—and they're right. Only, they don't understand this dry country, where a steer walks a rod for a blade of grass, and a hundred square miles supports one outfit. When they think of the west they think of some place like Montana, where you can fence a whole herd on five sections of grass and watch 'em thrive. They don't know Arizona, Nevada—West Utah, South Oregon—all this country where the roads peter out, and the horse picks up where the roads leave off— this country they never see. If you told 'em that there's 500,000 square miles that can't carry eight head of cattle to the square mile, they'd say you lied. Marian can't believe her own eyes—didn't smart people tell her

34

different, back east? Or else she thinks this must be just a lost place, where us backward people got stranded. She can't see her 94 as part and parcel of half a million miles of range."

"*Her* 94?" Wheeler questioned.

Horse Dunn did not hear him. "I've fought this country since time out of mind. When you got enemies in this country you've got to rough 'em and force 'em. If a man tries to smash you, you got to smash him first. She tells me we got law here to take care of that, nowdays. I tell you the law we got hasn't the teeth in it that it had in the old days, even!"

"Is Walt Amos a crook?"

"Anybody can run Walt Amos that can show a handful of votes. Marian doesn't understand that. She thinks I can run to Walt Amos and get everything fixed up. I tell you that ain't the way!" Dunn's big voice fairly crackled. "You got to drive 'em and blast 'em—keep their respect. Show weakness and they'll close in on you like wolves turn and eat the first wolf to go down."

Wheeler was silent. He could not altogether agree with Horse Dunn. He had seen range quarrels settled by gunfire—but never to the advantage of either winner or loser. However, he wasn't going to argue with the Old Man.

"What if she ties my hands?" Dunn demanded. "I've got to fight this thing my own way. For myself I wouldn't so much mind. But ain't the outfit hers, to begin with?"

"Hers?" Wheeler repeated.

"Sure, it's hers. Didn't you know that?"

Wheeler had not known it. "But look here! You've run this brand ever since I can remember. You must at least have some part interest here."

"Not a penny or a head of stock," Dunn told him.

"But I happen to know," Wheeler declared, "that you've always had an outfit, another outfit, down in Arizona. Yet your Arizona outfit hasn't seen you four times in a dozen years."

"I've had my hands full here," Dunn said.

"You mean," Billy Wheeler said, "you spent the last twelve-thirteen years neglecting your own outfit to build up a brand that don't belong to you?"

Dunn shrugged. "Somebody had to take holt. My brother died—sudden. He didn't leave the 94 in very good shape. For two years it was run by different bosses I hired. But this same Link Bender—he had a big outfit then—he was stealing the 94 blind. Pretty soon there wouldn't have been any 94. And it was all the kid and her mother had."

Billy Wheeler stared at Horse Dunn. Once he had heard it rumored that Horse Dunn had loved Marian's mother, long ago. In support of this theory now stood the silent testimony of Dunn's twelve years of unflagging devotion to an outfit not his own, while he carried on his dead brother's brand.

"Marian's mother always hated and feared this country. She brought up Marian to feel some similar. That's why the kid can't stand gunsmoke, or anything done by force. You see—my brother died with a gun in his hand."

Wheeler was silent. All the time while the Old Man raved he had been trying to think of a good way to tell Horse Dunn that he could not help him here; but now he saw that they had him. If Horse Dunn was put out of action, legally or otherwise, Wheeler could not trust the fortunes of the brand to unknown hands.

"I've tried to build her a real cow kingdom," Horse

36

Dunn growled. "If I can get the 94 over this hump Marian will never have a worry. But the way things stand—I don't know."

Wheeler said, "You set considerable store by this girl, don't you?"

Horse Dunn suddenly turned, and studied him curiously. "I don't know," he said after a moment, "but what you do too."

"Maybe I do." For a moment they looked at each other oddly, poker-faced.

"She ties our hands," Horse Dunn said. "So far as she's concerned, we can't win. If we whip this thing the only way it can be whipped—she'll hate us from here out. You realize that?"

"We got to think of the brand," Wheeler said.

"We're coming into gunsmoke, Billy. And after the smoke clears—you're going to find this girl is not for you."

"No," Wheeler said; "she's not for me." They were silent a minute.

Wheeler, unable to endorse the Old Man's leaning toward violence, expressed a belief that there ought to be some way to avoid smoking up the range. "If we can hold the 94 steady on the finance side," he said, "what can Link Bender's crowd do?"

"God knows I've took all the steps I know to steady the finance side," Horse Dunn said. "A minute ago you spoke of my having an outfit in Arizona. Well, I *had* an outfit in Arizona. Six weeks ago I sent word to Bob Flagg, my partner there, to sell her out. She's sold. For the last ten days I've been looking for Bob Flagg. He's supposed to show here with fifty thousand, as good as in cash; another fifty thousand in different obligations and notes. Everything I've got goes to the bracing of the

37

94."

Wheeler said slowly, "Was that necessary, Horse?"

"As soon as we get a chance I'll go through the books with you—you may be running this outfit pretty quick. You'll see what I saw months ago—the money from the Arizona brand just does give us a fighting chance. Without it—no chance at all."

"When does Flagg get here?"

Horse Dunn showed a sudden burst of exasperation. "Who knows when Bog Flagg gets any place? It's been all I could do to get two letters a year out of him. It beats a man to know what he's doing or how he's going at it. I have word that he sold out for me, like I told you. But where is he now? *Quien sabe!* I sent five wires and got no reply. If I don't lift his everlasting hide—" He fell silent.

He was staring out the open doorway toward the corrals; and now Billy Wheeler saw Horse Dunn's rocky face slowly relax, and soften. Out at the far corral Marian had caught the quiet old pony that Horse had given her, and was preparing to saddle. Horse Dunn watched her, his eyes gentle. There was always a shy humility about that strapping big old man when he looked at this girl, this daughter of his dead brother. It was almost as if he might have been looking at his own daughter, who had grown up away from him. After all, she might have been his daughter, if things had broken differently once.

"You go ride with her," Dunn said with a certain awkwardness. "You talk to her. Try to make her see that—that this is a—a different country, kind of."

"She doesn't take any stock in me, Horse."

"You go, anyway," Dunn insisted. "I don't like to have her riding this big range alone." With a curious reluctance Wheeler picked up his hat and walked out to

38

the stable where his saddle was.

CHAPTER SIX

A RISE OF DUST WAS GOING UP ON THE INSPIRATION road as Wheeler saddled; he knew the approaching car must be driven by Steve Hurley. For a moment he hesitated, for he would have liked to hear the latest word from the camp of Horse Dunn's enemies. Marian Dunn, however, was loping eastward along an old trail not far off the Inspiration road. Steve Hurley would be able to signal to him from road to trail if any new word concerned him. He let his pony lope out and caught up with Marian within the mile.

"Do you mind if I ride your way?"

"Maybe," Marian said, "you'll show me where Short Creek is."

Wheeler was startled. "Short Creek?"

"Sornetimes," the girl said, "it's easier to look at a thing than to imagine it. I know that Short Creek is just some little quiet shallows in a cut bank, where cattle come to drink; and the sun shines on it, and it looks like any other little desert creek. But I want to look at it—to kind of assure myself of all that. Sometimes your imagination makes a dreadful thing of a place where such things can happen."

Wheeler was troubled; partly because he suddenly perceived how sensitively the girl had reacted to a happening which he himself had regarded only as a practical nuisance; but partly too because it made him foolishly uneasy to think of Marian riding alone in that quarter of the range.

"I was thinking some of riding over that way," he
39

conceded. "Only—I wish you'd let somebody know when you set off to ride a distance like that, so somebody could go with you."

She looked at him sidelong for a minute. "Sometimes it seems to me you people do everything you can to make this into an unfriendly country."

"I don't know what you mean."

"These Red Hills, with the sun on them, are the background of the very earliest memories I have. When I came here again it was as if I were coming home. I felt free and natural, here—at first. And Horse Dunn is almost exactly like my father, what little I can remember of him—so nearly like my father that I can't remember my father's face any more; because my uncle's face comes in between."

"He worships the ground you walk on," Wheeler said.

"I know." A little shiver ran across her shoulders, anomalous in the blaze of the sun. "Then he turns and does some wild, awful thing like yesterday; and it gives me the strangest feeling of being completely lost in a country I don't understand."

"Yesterday? What awful thing?"

"He—he shot Link Bender."

"It was kind of unfortunate, sure. But I don't know what else he could do. Link drew on him. And all your uncle did was to nick him in the arm, so that he dropped the gun."

Marian's tone was curiously detached, unforgiving. "He admitted he set out to goad Link Bender into fighting."

That was not exactly what Horse Dunn had said, but essentially the girl was right. It was like Horse Dunn too that he could in no part lie to this girl, but would put himself conscientiously into the worst possible light.

"He said more," Marian added. "He said that if it hadn't been for me he would have killed Link Bender there at Chuck Box Wash."

Billy Wheeler started to say, "Oh, I don't think—" It was no use. It was futile to try to hide from this girl certain things which she was in no way equipped to understand, yet was sure to see clearly. "This is a different country than you're used to, Marian. Dry country men learned long ago to depend on themselves; they've lived that way for a long time."

"You're trying to justify—shooting down a man?"

He had an answer for that. But before he answered he looked at her for a moment—with the result that he did not answer at all. Marian Dunn sat her horse gracefully, with a fine natural balance; if she had been raised in this country she would have been a fine horsewoman— would be yet, given a year or two in the saddle. And to Billy Wheeler she seemed, as always, the loveliest thing he had ever seen; the more so because she was manifestly of a different, far-off world, a world kindlier and more gentle than his own. She had the magic of the distant unknown, and the blue of distance was in her eyes.

But he could not forget that he had ridden with this girl many times before, stirrup to stirrup as now; and in the end had hoped never to ride with her again. Having failed of persuasion in his own behalf, what was the use of his trying to plead the case of Horse Dunn?

The car that had been an approaching funnel of dust upon the Inspiration road now came careening around a rutty bend two hundred yards below them. Steve Hurley leaned from behind his dusty windshield to wave at them, then brought his car to a long-rolling stop. He signaled Wheeler to ride to him.

41

"Wait here," Wheeler said to the girl. He wheeled his horse, then hesitated to say over his shoulder, "Don't worry; we'll work everything out all right."

He put his horse down to the road, jumping it through the red rocks. From behind the wheel Steve Hurley thrust a big square hand at him, and Steve's big beefy face flashed a quick grin. "Glad to see you, Billy; the Old Man said he figured you'd sit in. As soon as I see who it was, I pulled up."

Wheeler glanced at the boiling radiator. "What's broke in Inspiration, Steve?"

"The Old Man may be wanting to call his riders in. Thought I'd stop and tell you what it was, so's you could signal in any of the boys you might see while you're out."

"I'm listening."

"It's all over Inspiration that Sheriff Walt Amos will make an arrest within three days. They're saying the sheriff knows who's dead; that it's a man Dunn swore to kill if ever he found him on 94 range." Steve Hurley's sun-squinted eyes rested steadily and keenly on Billy Wheeler.

"Steve," said Wheeler, "will Horse Dunn submit to arrest?"

Steve Hurley looked away a moment before he answered. "I don't know," he said at last. "But I guess maybe. Am I right he'll want his riders in?"

"I'd sure think so. This thing is coming faster than I figured it would, Steve."

Hurley half grinned on one side of his face, grimly. "There might be a couple of other folks surprised before the week it out." He clashed his gears, the dust snorted from under his tires, and he was gone.

The girl's eyes were questioning as Billy Wheeler

returned to her side. "Don't worry," he said; "it's all going to work out."

They turned off, no longer paralleling the Inspiration road; and for a long while as the miles slowly unrolled under the fox-trotting hoofs of the ponies neither had anything to say. Wheeler was schooling himself to accept the fact that although they were riding stirrup to stirrup again, he must not again make love to her, nor sing to her, nor even look at her unless she spoke, lest new strength be given the bitterness of his old defeat.

They were near Short Creek when the girl spoke unexpectedly. "I'm glad you came. You make things seem straighter and smoother, just the way you pace your horse along, without any worry or fret."

"There isn't anything to worry about."

"You've changed since two years ago," the girl told him. "Somehow you're nicer to ride with—quieter, more restful."

He glanced at her but didn't answer.

"You used to be a stampedey sort of person," she explained, "always rushing your horse at things. Whatever you went at, you always went at it the same way—thunder of hoofs, taking all obstacles by storm. I think I used to be afraid of you."

For a moment he wondered if things would have gone differently between them if he had been less eager, less turbulent. When you wanted a thing too much you overplayed your hand and lost out altogether. Maybe you could love a girl too much, too soon, and defeat yourself the same way. Perhaps if—

A quarter of a mile away within the sharp-cut bed of Short Creek something moved, held steady a moment, then disappeared. It was a rider there, who was watching them; but it was not a rider who meant to rise

43

in his stirrups and hail.

"Well," he said briskly, "this is Short Crick. You've seen it now. This is about all there is to it—just a crick running along in the dry. I think we'd better be pushing back now; it'll pretty soon be time to eat."

"I came out here to see where this thing happened," Marian said with an unexpected stubbornness. "I don't expect to go back until I've been shown."

"You insist on that?"

"I absolutely do."

He hesitated, trying to estimate who the now concealed rider might be and what might be the purpose of his concealment, but he could not. For a moment he wondered whether he had not better get Marian away from there at all cost; but he did not wish to risk conveying to her that anything to be feared or dreaded could be here. He led out a quick lope, anxious to get it over with.

"This," he said, pulling up his horse at the spot the cattle had trampled, "is nothing but a place where it just happened that somebody took a shot at somebody. What is there to see? Nothing. I want you to think of this place as just a crick where horses come to drink."

Marian Dunn sat very quiet, staring at the shallow water. He wondered what things, terrible to her, she might be picturing.

"I'm glad I came," Marian said. "But especially I'm glad you came. You—"

"Listen," he said.

A horse as yet unseen was coming fast down the cut. Its unshod hoofs padded quietly in the sand at the margin of the water, so that its thudding lope was sensed less by sound than by shock—the faint distant tremor of the ground.

44

"What is it?" the girl asked.

"Don't you hear? A horse is coming up."

"I don't—" she started to say that she didn't hear anything; but just then the unseen rider cut through the shallows with a sudden sharp sound of thrown water and the ring of hoofs on stone. "Who is it?"

"*Quien sabe?* Turn and ride back the way we've come," he told her without emphasis. "I'll be along in a minute."

"But why? Who is it?"

"I don't know who it is. He kept himself out of sight and didn't hail, is all I know. I've been watching him for fifteen minutes."

"For fifteen minutes? But you didn't say anything."

"Please do as I say. If I knew who this was I'd tell you. I'll have to ask you to do as I say anyway. Turn your horse and send him into a lope."

A queer expression came into the girl's eyes. "This sort of thing gives me a strange creepy feeling. Why don't you tell me what's the matter?"

"Because I don't know, I tell you. Are you going or not?"

Without a word Marian turned her horse; she was at the two hundred yards as a hard-run horse surged up over the lip of the cut. The rider was Kid Bender.

The Kid half wheeled his pony, drove close to Billy Wheeler's horse; his lean figure swayed backwards as he brought his pony to a sliding stop, very close. Across the back of his right hand showed the heavy purple welt that Wheeler's quirt had laid there; and in his face was the joyous anger of a man who takes payment for a past humiliation.

"What you doing here?"

Wheeler ignored the question. "You're a little off

45

your range, Kid," he said. "This range comes under the head of the 94. Maybe I'll be ordering you off it pretty quick. I haven't decided yet."

"No," said Kid Bender. "I don't think you will. You're dealing with a peace officer—patroling the scene of a crime."

"Peace officer?"

Kid Bender flipped over the tail end of his neckerchief to reveal a nickel-plated shield. It was cheap and it was new; but as it flashed in the sun Wheeler felt his scalp stir oddly, as if he had glimpsed fire behind smoke. Horse Dunn's view of the situation was shaping up faster than Horse himself had imagined.

"Yesterday," said the Kid, "you knocked a gun out of my hand."

Billy Wheeler said distinctly, "With a quirt. I whipped it out of your hand with a quirt."

Kid Bender's face darkened for an instant but the hard gleam of a joyous anticipation immediately returned to his eye. "I have orders," he said, "to see that the hired men of the 94 don't trample over the scene of this crime any more. I'm starting with you; I'll give you fellers something to remember orders by. I'm taking your horse and your gun. Maybe your girl there will give you a lift after you're afoot. Or maybe I'll send her on home—I haven't decided that yet."

"No," said Wheeler, "you're not taking either horse or gun."

"You're against an officer of the law. You know what that means?"

"I know," Billy Wheeler said, "what I hope it means."

For a moment Kid Bender hesitated; they sat watching each other, two men in a situation from which neither could withdraw. One of them had sought this

46

meeting—the other welcomed it. Both knew that something peculiarly personal had to be settled here, now, between the two of them alone.

"I see your girl has stopped a little way up here," the Kid said; "seems like she sets watching from the hill."

Wheeler suppressed in time an impulse to glance over his shoulder. Instead his eyes never left Kid Bender as he jerked his chin sharply toward his shoulder as if he glanced away.

Kid Bender's quirt-marked hand flashed to his gun. For the second time in two days Wheeler forgot his own unaccustomed weapon. The horses were neck to neck, facing each other; and now Wheeler, slamming the rowels into his own pony, grabbed at the spade bit of Kid Bender's horse.

Kid Bender's gun exploded skyward as the Kid's horse reared straight up, driven over backwards by the plunge of Wheeler's pony against the cruel bit. For an instant Bender's pony fought for its balance on its hind legs. Then together horse and man went down.

Wheeler whirled his pony aside; and now he drew at last, and turned the muzzle of his cocked gun upward, ready.

Bender's horse struggled up and bolted, bucking against the loosened saddle; but the man lay quiet where he had gone down.

CHAPTER SEVEN

VAL DOUGLAS, WAGON BOSS FOR THE 94, LEANED against the red rock fireplace of the main room of the ranch house, and looked at Billy Wheeler without admiration. "Now you've done it," he said; "oh, you've done it now, all right!"

Billy Wheeler sat down, stretched his long legs in front of him and fixed his grey gaze upon Douglas without expression. Val Douglas was tall and lean, blue-eyed, but black of brows and hair; he was a crack rider, a crack roper, a good man on any cow range. Ordinarily Billy Wheeler would have got along well with such a man—and he understood now why Val Douglas disliked him. Already Wheeler had noticed that it was hard for Douglas to keep his eyes from following Marian Dunn whenever she was in view. And it was Val Douglas who most often saddled Marian's horse, rode with her on the desert trails.

"I won't ask you what you'd have done in my place," Wheeler said, "because I don't give a hoot. But I'll say this—if you had done much differently it would be because you're a worse fool than I thought."

It was many hours now since Billy Wheeler had upset Kid Bender's horse, pinning that newly-made deputy sheriff under the saddle; the long peculiarly lucid twilight of the Red Hills country now lay cool and lingering upon the range. But report of the clash with Kid Bender had been delayed by Horse Dunn's absence.

Horse Dunn and his wagon boss had now heard the story of the order Kid Bender had given Wheeler, and Wheeler's refusal; and of how the Kid had tried to trick Wheeler into glancing away while he drew. There had been a bad moment for Wheeler after he had overthrown the Kid's horse, for at first Kid Bender had looked as if he might be dead, saddle-crushed by his fallen mount.

Kid Bender, though, had come to with only a broken leg and a dirty crack on the head to show. And Pinto Halliday, shifty-eyed, lanky, had appeared from the

Short Creek cuts to take Kid Bender off of Wheeler's embarrassed hands. Halliday, it appeared, was another newly-made deputy. Evidently he had been the other half of the Short Creek patrol.

"No show-off play like that ever does any good," Douglas said. "It only stacks trouble onto plenty we already got."

At the window Horse Dunn stirred impatiently. It was characteristic of Dunn that whenever he was found inside a house, it was always at a window looking out, as a restless horse stares out through the bars of a corral. "Understand this, Val," he said. "Billy done just what I would have done in a like case. I'll back Billy's play to the limit, and that goes for any other play he wants to make!"

"Sure," said Douglas. "What else can we do?"

Wheeler sat up, angering again. "Now just a minute!"

Horse Dunn whirled. "Cut it out," he snapped. "Val, that was Old Man Coffee just come in; go take care of his horse, and see that there's grub laid out at the cook shack."

When Val Douglas had gone out Billy Wheeler's anger left him. "He's mostly right, Horse," he said.

Horse Dunn bristled and his voice rose to its familiar roar. "All I'm sorry for is you didn't kill the little sneak! If I had a couple more riders with enough guts in their bellies to—" His thunder subsided; again Wheeler noticed how all the hard fire went out of this old man in the presence of his niece. Marian Dunn sat relaxed at the other window, her eyes in the far hills, and her profile was as motionless as if she were carved of cream-colored marble. Billy Wheeler had that day seen horror and antipathy in her eyes after he had downed Kid Bender; and he no longer wondered why Horse

49

Dunn lost spirit sometimes when she was there.

Horse Dunn mumbled in obscure apology, "We're right sorry. Things sometimes go like this. But sometimes we can't help it if they do. If only Bob Flagg would get here—"

Marian Dunn gave no sign of having heard, and there was an awkward silence. Then Old Man Coffee came stalking across from the corrals, dropped a saddle from his hip to the gallery floor, and let himself in.

"Val Douglas says that Billy Wheeler, here, stirred up a little extra hell today," he said without preliminaries.

Horse Dunn grunted, and Wheeler briefly explained to the old lion hunter what had happened.

"Well," Old Man Coffee said, "I reckon Marian can testify she seen him go for his gun."

Marian did not verify this. After a moment Horse Dunn said, "I suppose you didn't find anything, or you'd be saying so."

"I'd sure like to catch up with that Cayuse Cayetano," Coffee said. "Today I seen him riding a horse to death, some northward, toward the Red Sleep. I'd sure like to know what he was at."

"You worry plenty about that Indian, don't you? If—"

"He knows too much, too soon," Coffee complained. "Why wasn't he promoting the Short Crick trails, like me? Something funny about this Cayuse, Horse."

"So you lost out," Horse accused him.

Old Man Coffee eased himself onto the most uncomfortable chair in the room, and there draped himself angularly. "If there's anything in the world makes me mad," he said morosely, "it's a cussed fool hound."

The droop-eared old lion dog which had followed Coffee in looked at him mournfully, and flopped to the

50

floor with a great rattle of elbows, but made no remark. "I set out to trail the killer's horse," Coffee went on. "I took off down-crick; Rock seeking the trail where it come out of the water. Pretty soon he says he's got it, and sets up a beller, and away we go, inching along about two miles an hour. That fool hound takes me anyway six, eight miles, all the time hollering just as confident as if he knew what he was at."

Old Man Coffee crammed cut plug into an ancient pipe, the bowl of which was carved to represent hearts and flowers.

"Well?" Dunn demanded at last .

"All this time," Coffee said, "I hadn't been able to make out a decent track; but I was getting kind of suspicious because of the way the trail wandered around. Then finally we come on a soft place, where I could see plain. And it was the wrong trail."

"I thought this dog couldn't be fooled," Dunn grunted.

"He was sure fooled this time. The trail your wagon boss showed me was off a cup-hoofed pony; the hoofs showed nail splits. But old Rock took after a pony that was flat-footed as a duck—his feet wore down right onto the frog."

"So," Horse Dunn said, "you ended up empty-handed, same as us ordinary folks!"

"Not altogether and complete," Coffee retorted. "Rock quit cold—wouldn't work no more. But I took and unraveled the other trail by hand." He stepped out onto the gallery and came back with the saddle, which he now threw down among them in a tangle of broken strappage. "There," he said casually, "is the death saddle you was inquiring after."

Billy Wheeler heard Marian's breath jerk through her

51

teeth. In the failing light her eyes looked surprisingly dark.

"Good Lord!" said Dunn. "How'd you lay hands on that?"

"Why, I followed the trail of the dead man's horse, until I come to the place he rolled loose from it. How'd you suppose?"

Horse Dunn had dropped to his knees beside the saddle. None of them had realized how deep the room was in twilight until it was brightened by the flare of the match he struck. For a long moment Horse Dunn studied the old worn leather, until the flame burned to his finger tips and went out. He stood up slowly. "You know that saddle?"

"No," said Wheeler. "Do you?"

Behind Horse Dunn's shaggy face the muscles were stiffening slowly, so that although his features remained in some sense a mask, his eyes presently began to gleam with the white heat of the anger which he could not repress. "Yes," he said.

Yet he did not immediately answer their unspoken question. He turned to the window again, and for a little while stood looking out as if he could not yet trust himself to speak. Out behind the barns, Coffee's five other hounds were churning the quiet twilight with mournful bellowings, and for a little while they all seemed to be listening to that. Then Marian got up and went quietly from the room, and for once her uncle seemed glad to have her go.

"Here they're setting out to put the hooks to me," Horse Dunn said at last—"hunting a strangle holt on my brand. And it's a shameful thing that this should come onto us because somebody rubbed out maybe the most worthless character that ever rode the Red Hills range."

"You know the name?" said Old Man Coffee.

"What's his name matter?" Horse Dunn exploded. "His name was Lon Magoon—and what of it? A cow thief—in a small, cheap way. He'd go around on different ranges, and he'd steal a beef here, and another there; skin 'em and sell 'em to some butcher a hundred miles away for half price."

"Horse," said Coffee, "who would have killed this man?"

"Anybody!" Horse Dunn roared. "Any cowman with enough guts to rub out a cow thief! I ought to've killed him myself last time I caught him with the carcass of a 94 cow!"

"Did you know he was operating on this range?"

"What's the difference if I did or not? We know it now. Billy, you take that saddle, and kick it under my bunk!"

"You better turn it in to the sheriff, Horse," Coffee said. "You'll be suppressing evidence if you keep it here."

"Damned if I will!" Horse Dunn said. "All they want is to hang this thing on the 94—on me. You think I called you in to help 'em? No, by God!"

He flung himself into a chair, his eyes incandescent above the short shag of his beard. Coffee and Bill Wheeler looked at each other, amazed at the violence of the Old Man's bitterness.

"Go get yourself something to eat," Dunn growled. "You going to keep Tia waiting all night?"

They went out and left him sitting there. He was still sitting there an hour later when Tulare Callahan came in.

CHAPTER EIGHT

TULARE CALLAHAN WAS A SMALL MAN, VERY WIRY, with a cheerfully hard face. He had relieved Steve Hurley, who for three days had kept an eye on the state of affairs at the county seat of Inspiration, and he now came roaring into the 94 layout in Horse Dunn's heavy old touring car. He was grinning with the delight of an action-hungry man who smells smoke at last.

"I hear Billy Wheeler like to murdered a guy," said he. "Billy Wheeler slapped Kid Bender with a horse," Dunn said. "You come all the way back here to tell us that?"

"I thought maybe you might want to hear the upshot," Tulare said. "The sheriff's coming out to get Wheeler, either tonight or first thing in the morning. He's going to throw him in the jug. Did you know that?"

"No," Horse Dunn said, "I didn't know that. And I don't know it yet."

"Well, I'm just telling you what he says.

"What he thinks he's going to do, and what is actually going to take place—that may still yet be two different things," Horse growled.

"Kid Bender is at his pa's ranch," Tulare went on. "From what I hear, he got there feeling very poorly— might not even have made it without help. He has one leg busted, and a couple ribs; and it seems he busted a rock with his bean. Link Bender's in town. Seems like he's offended about something; it may be he doesn't take this kindly."

"What's the charge against Billy?" Horse asked.

"Assault with a deadly weapon."

54

"Billy didn't assault him with anything!"

"The heck he didn't," Old Man Coffee put in. "Didn't he hurl the Kid's horse at him?"

"The town is full of small-time cowmen and their professional calf thieves," Tulare reported. "Seems like every guy in the country that has it in for the 94 is swarming into Inspiration. I bet there's twenty guys that's tried to get themselves made deputies. If Walt Amos called for a posse he could easy raise a hundred men."

Horse Dunn blew a slow smoke cloud, and sat staring through it with a small grim smile on his face. His eyes were deep in distance, so deep that he might have been staring across the desert to the far-flung limits of the 94 cow kingdom. That was a range of bitter struggles, fought the harder because the poverty of the feed made it necessary for each brand to control vast areas; and across the gaunt Red Hills the 94 had advanced year by year like creeping sands. Horse Dunn had proved himself a hard man—a hard fighter, a hard trader, a hard enemy. He had never once hesitated to make a bitter enemy to gain for the property of his niece one more mile of range. Val Douglas, Old Man Coffee, Tulare, Billy Wheeler—all of them knew that. Only Marian Dunn, quiet in the shadows, knew nothing of how embattled Horse Dunn had been for more than a decade—in her behalf.

"So they figure to arrest Billy Wheeler," Dunn said.

"They can't hold him," Coffee said. "I suppose Kid Bender will run into Pinto Halliday as a witness, and they'll all lie to beat the cards. But what good will it do 'em? Marian was there. Billy's got a witness that can make a fool of 'em in any court in the world."

Marian Dunn said, almost under her breath but very

clearly, "I can't testify."

Horse Dunn looked startled. "What's that?" he demanded.

"I didn't see anything," Marian said. "I don't know how the fight started. Billy just suddenly jumped his horse at the other horse, and it went over backward. That's all I saw."

Horse Dunn turned to her. He seemed puzzled, but very quiet. "Marian," he said, "didn't you hear Billy tell what happened? How Kid Bender went for his gun?"

The girl said, "Yes, I heard him."

"I've known Billy Wheeler since he had to shin up a horse's leg to get on. You think he'd lie to us here?"

"No; I didn't say I thought he lied."

"Then what's to stop you from backing him up?"

In the girl's eyes showed something Billy Wheeler had never seen there before. Her face was as gentle and lucid as the face of a child; but though her eyes were troubled there was a sober strength behind them as immutable in its way as the rocky will of Horse Dunn. She seemed to be looking into something terribly sad, but completely inevitable; she faced it without excitement and without flinching. "I can't swear to something I didn't see."

Horse Dunn looked at her, then turned away and let his hands fall in a gesture of utter futility. His eyes turned to Billy Wheeler. "You see?" he said. "You see?"

Old Man Coffee broke the awkward pause. "Look here," he said. "There's something about this I don't get. Yesterday you shot Link Bender through the arm, Horse, right before the sheriff's eyes. Nothing comes of that. How is it the sheriff lets that pass, yet jumps in with both feet the minute Billy Wheeler raises his hand

56

in self defense?"

Marian Dunn unexpectedly addressed her uncle. "There—you see? Isn't that what I've been trying to tell you? There *is* law and justice, even here. Evidently the sheriff saw that Link Bender was first to draw—that's why he made no arrest in your case, Uncle John. He doesn't have that evidence in Billy's case, so of course he has to make the arrest."

"I'm not so sure," Coffee said.

"You want to know the answer?" Horse Dunn demanded. "He didn't take me because he hasn't got the guts to take me. What, haul me in on a charge like that? He knows it can't be done! What he fails to allow for now is that the 94 will back Billy Wheeler just the same as if he'd been here all his life. When he finds that out you'll see him drop back!"

"I'm not so sure," said Old Man Coffee again.

"You're not sure? Look at it, man!"

"I am looking at it. Seems like to me, Horse, the game is a little different from that. He may be laying off of you because his crowd has a little different plans for you. I'll say right here, this sure makes it look to me like they must have a case against you on the murder of Lon Magoon—a case we maybe can begin worrying about."

"Then why do they turn and jump on Billy Wheeler?"

"It might be because Billy Wheeler is kind of strong as a cattleman. I'm speaking of bank strength. I don't know anything about how Billy Wheeler stands in this mess. But it may be they think he might work out as an ace card in patching up the finances of the 94. That being the case, naturally they'd like nothing better than to set him aside to cool for thirty days. A man can't read his facts unless he looks a little into the people situation. It sure begins to look," said Old Man Coffee, "as if I'm

57

going to have to go to Inspiration for this trial."

"No," said Horse Dunn. "Because there isn't going to be any trial."

Marian Dunn said sharply, "What do you mean?"

For once Horse Dunn failed to wilt before the flare-up of his niece. "I won't stand for it," he declared. "I've stood enough! They'll take Billy Wheeler no place."

"You can't do that!" Marian cried out. "Do you think you can stand up against the law? You can't—"

"Damn the law!" Dunn thundered. "Where would this brand be today if I'd left it to them and the law? I'd have lost the range four times to sheep, three times under twisted land laws no better than blackmail. To say nothing of being swarmed over every year by this eternal coyote ring that don't know how to use the range when they get it. Half the battle has been the crooked meddling of so-called law!"

"But—"

Her uncle fairly shouted her down. "They say I forced them out. They say I roughed the range, hoolihanned the little brands. Range-hog is the name they use. But I tell you I paid for every water hole, every range right—paid in full. I bought out outfits that were broke and worse than broke, when nobody else would buy. But they want their pay and the range too. By God, I'll show them range roughing! I'll show them hoolihan! I'll—"

"I think," Marian Dunn said, "you must be mad!"

"Mad, is it? Mad or no mad, the coyote pack will never take Billy Wheeler in."

"There's this about it, Mr. Dunn," Val Douglas drawled. "We're coming up against bigger things here than an open fight over whether or not this Wheeler will stand up and take his medicine for busting the Kid's leg. After all, there's something in what your niece says.

Tulare says that tonight or tomorrow Amos can raise up a posse of a hundred. We'd look good trying to bronc-stomp a hundred men."

"A hundred soap kettles! I don't believe there's three men in the bunch." Dunn studied his wagon boss narrowly. "Val, what's come over you?"

"Nothing's come over me. I only say—"

Horse Dunn bellowed, "You stand there and tell me—"

Billy Wheeler cut in. "He's right, Horse."

"*What?*"

Billy Wheeler looked Val Douglas over coolly. "Val doesn't strike me like a feller that would be right very often," he said at last. "But this ought to raise his percentage, I guess. I'm going to leave 'em take me, Horse."

"You'll do nothing of the kind," Horse Dunn told him. "I'm boss here!"

Billy Wheeler sprawled relaxed, as if he were resting, and met Dunn's glare evenly. If the others there did not understand why the Old Man of the 94 turned to this youngster more readily than to any one else in time of need, they could have learned something about that by looking at them now.

"I don't know as you can stop me, Horse," Wheeler said.

Horse Dunn did not give in at once. That old man was from other wilder times; and his tremendous robust vitality, which made it seem as if an Indian medicine kept him from growing old, upheld in him the embattled spirit of his youth. He had been young when the country was young, and perhaps the country had changed more readily than he. Never in his life had he gained anything by bending; always he had stood and fought for his

59

own. Now, in the unacknowledged advance of his age, it was a bitter thing for him to bend even a little way. But Wheeler was right in one thing: if Wheeler meant to submit to trial, Horse Dunn couldn't stop him.

So Dunn gave in at last. He ran a big hand through his thinned roan hair. "How long? Oh Lord, how long! If only Bob Flagg would come . . ."

The day was hardly breaking when Sheriff Walt Amos came hammering at the door.

CHAPTER NINE

THE SHERIFF CAME ALONE , WITHOUT SHOW OF FORCE. Wheeler's surrender he outwardly took as a matter of course; though a close observer might have detected a certain pleased relief.

It was nearly six in the morning as they rolled down the dusty ruts toward the first test of strength since the killing at Short Creek. Three cars drove to Inspiration, for Billy Wheeler had reserved certain privileges of free action; and the sheriff returned to Inspiration alone in his own car, as he had come. A second car was driven by Horse Dunn, who took with him Gil Baker, Steve Hurley, and Tulare Callahan; and—what seemed more important—Marian Dunn, between Val Douglas and her huge uncle in the front seat. The Old Man of the 94 was possessed by a vague persistent hope that somewhere, some time, Marian would see something which would change leer opinions as to the balance of force and justice in the Red Hills ranges.

Old Man Coffee rode with Billy Wheeler, who drove his own roadster.

"There in that one car," said Coffee, watching Horse

60

Dunn's tower of dust, "goes all that's left of the 94 outfit; except for you and me, who don't really belong here."

Billy Wheeler nodded. "I couldn't hardly believe," he said, "that Horse was trying to run twenty thousand head of cattle, even through the quiet months, with only four men and himself."

"He's got twenty thousand head, has he?"

"The book count shows twenty thousand head. Allowing for death losses, he supposes he's got fourteen to sixteen thousand. Short-handed as he is, he can't be right sure."

"I've seen the day," Old Man Coffee said, "two, three years ago, when the 94 bunkhouse never held less than twelve or fifteen hands. And in roundup times I've seen better than fifty riders follow the 94 wagons. But I guess those days are gone."

"He thinks the cow business has gone to pieces because of too much fancy handling. He figures if you get enough range and enough cows on it, the thing ought to work itself out by main strength—like in the old days, when the Great Plains was open."

Coffee suggested that Horse Dunn was getting old. "It's hard for us old fellows to bend to new ways of handling cows—or men. Horse Dunn is like this old dog."

Between Old Man Coffee's knees sat his big black hound, old Rock. A grizzle of white hair salted old Rock's fore quarters. and though his body was still as cleanly molded as that of a young dog, his scarred old face showed the droop of age.

"Old Rock was boss of my pack for years," Coffee explained. "He showed the way, punished the pups into line. But a different, younger dog is pack boss now.

That's why old Rock has to be with me all the time, and make himself a nuisance—so's he'll feel he's above mixing with common dogs. Without that he'd die fighting or bust up the pack."

Old Man Coffee let his mild deep-set eyes wander over the Red Hills range. The twisting, deep-swinging road had to go a long way before it got off 94 territory.

"All us old fellers come to the same thing this old dog has come to," Coffee said. "Horse Dunn might just as well get ready to swaller that, like Rock, and like me. He's forced his way for a long time; but comes a time when he can't force it no more."

"And that," Wheeler said, "is what we've got to save him from. For God knows he'll never bow his head! It's up to you, more'n anybody."

"Don't count on me."

That was Old Man Coffee's attitude. Because of his uncommon sixth sense in handling a trail and because of his widely heard-of luck in making shrewd deductions, Old Man Coffee had been called in on many a mystery killing in the intermountain country. But though he worked hard without cost to anyone, he stubbornly avoided any official responsibility. "I got nothing to do with it." That was the Coffee theme song on a murder case.

But now he added, "Something's wrong. When I first looked at this case I thought it was open and shut. But something's the matter with this case. Somebody knows something they're not telling me."

Billy Wheeler waited, but the information which silence would have brought from most men was long in coming.

"People in this country is going to the dogs," Coffee complained. "Take you. Your old father had a pair of eyes that could find out the devil through the smoke of hell. But you—you ain't got any eyes. I not only got to do your thinking for you. I also got to see for you and hear for you and ride for you. I'll give you just a sample."

An ironic amusement faintly altered Old Man Coffee's gaunt face. This was where he got his fun out of life—making other people feel like fools. Coffee would wear himself out helping someone else without pay; and then, with a tongue like a horse rasp, do his best to get himself hated for his pains.

"Answer me one question," he said now. "What weapon killed Lon Magoon?"

Billy Wheeler looked at Coffee sidelong, and for a moment he hesitated. "Lon Magoon," he said, "was killed by a shotgun. Is that what you wanted to know?"

"Part. What else?"

"It was fired from in front of him, a little to his right-hand side, by a man on a horse."

"What else?"

"The shell was home-loaded. And that's all I know, yet."

Old Man Coffee was regarding Wheeler with a peculiar fixed expression. "Son," he said at last, "I back down; I'm free to admit I had you wrong. You're further along the trail than most of 'em. You got the shotgun right, at least. I suppose you seen that one shot pellet bogged into the seam of the leather on Lon Magoon's saddle horn?"

"Yes; I saw it."

"That little pellet is pretty well hid. I guess nobody saw it but you and me. But the rest of your dope's wrong. For one thing—Magoon wasn't killed by no man on a horse!"

63

"How do you know that?"

"How did you know the shell was home-loaded?"

"Because the charge was weak. The sign showed the horses was close together when the shot was fired. If the charge hadn't been weak that pellet of lead would have plowed a whole lot deeper than it did."

Old Man Coffee nodded approval. "A good catch," he said. "But I think you got it wrong. If the charge had been fired from close like you say, the killer could have rammed the long shotgun barrel plumb against Magoon—there wouldn't have been no shot in the saddle horn. It was *distance* slowed that pellet. Lon Magoon was shot by a third man, from up on the flat ground above the cut!"

"Seems like," Wheeler objected, "the trail of the third man should have showed up, somewhere about."

"Maybe; if it had been read proper before the cattle pawed out the sign. But—there's one man mixed into this that knows too much about trails to have left one himself—even if he'd been there. Son, did you think of that?"

Old Man Coffee's eyes were boring keenly into Billy Wheeler; Wheeler could feel those sharp old eyes, even though his own were on the road. Wheeler felt a wakening stimulation. He could see why the Piutes believed Old Man Coffee to have second sight. "Cayuse," he said. "Cayuse Cayetano—he might not leave a trail."

Coffee was silent.

"That changes things some," Wheeler said, "if you're right."

"You'll see two-three things change, son, before we're through."

"If we had time for a long fight—"

"I don't think it's going to be a long fight, son; I think it's all going to come quick and soon. I've only been here two days, Billy; you've been here only three. But there's some things can't go on long before something pops."

They fell silent, while the hard-working engine threw the rack of the road behind them in big spasms and gouts of dust; and far ahead presently showed the faint disturbance on the plain which was Inspiration.

Inspiration consisted principally of a main street, backed by a few score houses, some of them neatly painted, with a tree or two; many simply unpainted shacks. The main street itself somewhat outdid the town that backed it. It was unpaved, but it had a shriekingly modern brick business block, and twenty-five or thirty frame business buildings, all with wooden false fronts, many with wooden awnings which extended over the sidewalk.

To a stranger the town would not have seemed so full of people as Tulare Callahan's report perhaps suggested. But Billy Wheeler at once recognized a dozen or more cars which would not ordinarily have been there, and about an equal number of dozing cow ponies. And—as the 94 cars pulled up in front of the little frame building that housed the county office—Wheeler noticed a small inconspicuous stir in doorways, a too casual moving together of spur-heeled loungers at two or three places along the street.

Billy Wheeler caught Horse Dunn's signal as he slid his roadster to a stop. He stepped down from the wheel and walked forward to Dunn's car.

"We want to all kind of keep together, here, as we move into this," Horse Dunn said casually. "I don't think there's going to be any trouble of any kind. Still—

I wish Bob Flagg had got here. There aren't so many of us as there has been some years."

There had been a time, Billy Wheeler knew, when the 94, twenty or thirty cowboys strong, would not have hesitated to stand this town on its head. Once the 94 had been almost a minor hangout for the wild bunch, and people had claimed that no horse-and-gun disorder occurred within a week's ride without participation of a horse or two branded with the 94. For years it had been traditional that a 94 cowboy who was whipped in town could look for work elsewhere; and in some of these false fronts could still be found bullet holes commemorating the rampages of 94 cow hands of a Saturday night. Even yet the name of the brand alone should command a certain respect.

Glancing at Marian Dunn, Billy Wheeler saw that the girl's eyes were wide with appeal as they rested upon his; but he felt unable to respond. He supposed that she wanted him to try to keep her turbulent and ungovernable uncle out of war, but he found himself stiff and indifferent, eager for trouble, almost. Once he had offered this girl everything in his life, without arousing in her any emotion other than regret. Even now, today, she did not propose to speak in his behalf. And he resented the situation which kept him close to this girl who would never mean anything to him but disappointment and trouble.

But—as he met her eyes he knew that she was still the loveliest thing he had ever seen.

The sheriff pulled up and stepped to the sidewalk. Now that he was on his own ground again there was perceptible hardening and stiffening of the man; he did not look like the same peace officer who had so politely suggested, at daybreak, that Wheeler submit to trial in a peaceable way.

"Court won't open yet for a little bit," he said. "You, Wheeler, park yourself around here close. You're lucky not to be in the lock-up, by God! You, Dunn, I'll speak to you inside. I've got a couple of questions I figure to ask."

"All right," Horse Dunn said. "Come on, folks."

"The rest of you stay outside," Sheriff Amos said. "You're the one I aim to talk to, Dunn."

Horse Dunn looked up and down the street, noting how the groups of booted loungers had grown. Hardly a doorway in that street was empty now. Wheeler saw Dunn run a quick glance along the second story windows across the street. Dunn turned to his car, relaxed, casual.

"Marian, take this here car around the corner, and park it; then wait there, until someone brings word."

Marian glanced once, questioningly, at her uncle, then once more, almost despairingly, at Billy Wheeler. Then the car lumbered away in the dust as she obeyed.

Horse Dunn turned with a curious mildness to the sheriff. "I don't figure to give any answers, Amos, that I wouldn't just as leave my outfit would hear."

The Old Man of the 94 stood square-planted—smiling a little, almost bland; but the confidence of a lifelong dominance was in the easy set of his enormous shoulders, so that he seemed then bigger than the town, bigger than the range. All up and down that street were Link Bender's men—the sheriff's men—a hundred guns could be brought down on the old range boss with the first puff of smoke. Yet Sheriff Amos looked smaller, a badgered man, standing there in front of Horse Dunn. Flanking their Old Man, the cowboys of the 94 stood nonchalantly, spread out a little now; they watched three ways without seeming to watch. But it was Horse Dunn who stood like an immovable mountain. There was something in the old man that could break men down.

The sheriff hesitated; he knew what he was up against. Abruptly he burst out, "I decide these things here!"

The mild mask fell away. "Then give your orders to people you can boss," Dunn snarled at him.

CHAPTER TEN

SHERIFF WALT AMOS HESITATED. HORSE DUNN'S stand was senseless—the incredible sort of thing that was told of the men of the wild days. The town—the street—was full of the enemies of the 94. If the guns awoke it was certain that the young sheriff would be the first and surest to go down; but even if Dunn's people could somehow shoot their way clear, no possible outcome could win for them in the end. This was the peculiar thing about the self-dependent men from the old days, like Horse Dunn: time after time they waded obstinately ahead into sure disaster—instinctively confident that lesser men would draw back.

When Walt Amos had sized up the situation he stood for a moment with a blank face. Then—the young sheriff grinned, not sheepishly, and not irritably, but with the interested humor of a man who plays his own game against another's.

"Oh, all right, Dunn," he said; "I don't set any great store on that point. I haven't got any of my fellers with me—I don't need 'em; but maybe you need some. Bring 'em on!"

In effect, Horse Dunn had backed Sheriff Walt Amos

down; but Horse admitted afterward that it was here, in the backdown, that the young sheriff had first commanded his respect. He grunted an assent. "Billy Wheeler, Coffee—come on."

The others moved forward, but he waved them back; and Dunn, with Wheeler and Coffee, followed Amos into the little old adobe that held the sheriff's office. The sheriff sat down on the corner of a table that stood against one wall. "Have chairs, you people."

Old Man Coffee, who had the hunter's instinct for resting himself at every opportunity, sat down and shot tobacco juice at a sawdust box; but the boss of the 94 stood stubborn and balky in the middle of the floor, waiting.

"Dunn," said Sheriff Amos, "you were the first man found out there'd been a killing at Short Crick. That was Tuesday—three days ago. Right off you sent Tulare Callahan here, to wire Old Man Coffee, clear around at McTarnahan. Dunn, why did you send for Old Man Coffee?"

"I sent for Old Man Coffee," said Dunn, "to find out who was making free on my range. To tell you the truth, I didn't figure you numbskulls was equal to handling it."

"Then it wasn't your idea," said the sheriff, "to get him here to seize and suppress evidence?"

"When I want to seize something," Horse Dunn told him, "I won't be sending for some old guy the other side of two ranges of mountains. I'll just seize it."

"Where were you riding Monday, Dunn?"

"Monday I was riding Red Sleep Ridge."

"And when," the sheriff shot at him, "did you first learn that Lon Magoon was camping on 94 range?"

Horse Dunn did not hesitate for a fraction of a

69

second. "Yesterday—when Old Man Coffee found Magoon's saddle."

The sheriff's smooth, cornerless face tightened a little, but Billy Wbeeler saw that the man was not surprised. Instantly Wheeler knew two things. First, that one of the Inspiration crowd—perhaps with field glasses—must have seen Coffee pick the saddle up. And second, what was equally important, that the sheriff must have succeeded in tracing out the dead man's horse—and had identified it as belonging to the little cow thief, Magoon.

"Why," the sheriff demanded, "haven't you turned that saddle in to the authorities—to me?"

"Oh," said Horse Dunn with false innocence, "did you want that saddle?"

The sheriff hesitated, unexpectedly at a fading of the trail. For a moment he had undoubtedly believed he had trapped Horse; but this hope was now trampled out by doubts.

Old Man Coffee chuckled. "Son," he said to the young sheriff, "you gave away your hand when you put in that about seizing and compressing evidence. You couldn't jump no lion because your questions was headed the wrong way of the trail."

Sheriff Walt Amos studied him. "In short," he said, "you've got it in your mind that if I'd come at it different, Dunn would have denied he had Magoon's saddle!"

"You'll never know now, will you?" Coffee said.

Horse Dunn stood as expressionless as an adobe wall, and a dull color showed across the sheriff's cheek bones.

"One more question," said the sheriff. "I want to know where all your riders were, last Monday—the day

70

of the killing."

"Val Douglas and Gil Baker were on Yellow Medicine Flats; Steve Hurley and Tulare Callahan were riding Slinkard's Hole. That's all the riders I've got right now."

"Now leave me ask you one, sheriff," said Old Man Coffee. "S'long as we're on the question of whereats, where was Cayuse Cayetano?"

"When? Monday? Cayetano was prospecting up the Hungry Horse."

"Prospecting, huh?"

"Oh, I know he wasn't prospecting. I can't keep the Indian's from hunting deer out of season, and I don't pretend to."

"That is to say, you don't know where the hell he was!"

"Well, what of it?"

"That's very interesting," said Old Man Coffee.

"You finished with us?" Dunn demanded.

"One thing more," said the sheriff. "I questioned Hurley and Callahan when they were in town; but I still got to talk to Baker and Douglas. Stay here a minute."

At the door he turned and met Horse Dunn's eye squarely. "I don't mind telling you this," he said. "This case is nearly washed up. I figure to pick up the killer within sixty hours." He went out, jerking the door shut behind him.

Old Man Coffee's eyes showed an inward smile. "That last seemed kind of forced in," he said.

Horse took a turn up and down the room. He looked shaggy and gigantic, but he was as light on his long legs as a young buckaroo. "Now why," he said at last, "would Amos want to tell us that?"

Coffee regarded Horse Dunn pityingly. "Don't you

know?"

Gil Baker now lounged in, taking his time. The sheriff was impatient at his heels.

"Gil," said Horse Dunn, "the sheriff wants to know if you was really—"

"Hold your tongue!" Sheriff Amos snapped. He closed the door and leaned against it. "Baker, where were you Monday?"

Gil Baker, young and hawk-faced, glanced at Horse Dunn and rolled his quid of tobacco over his tongue. "Rode a scope of ground, last Monday," he offered.

"Mostly where?"

Baker watched the sheriff narrowly. "Mostly Slinkard's Hole."

"Anybody with you?"

"Part of the time."

The sheriff caught at this. "Douglas was with you only part of the time, huh?"

Gil Baker studied him, snake-eyed. "All the time," he changed his answer.

"You just said 'part of the time!'"

"My mistake," said Baker.

The young sheriff jerked open the door. "Val Douglas! Come in here!"

"You a poker player, son?" Old Man Coffee asked him.

"Maybe so, maybe not, but by God, I know the jack of spades when I see it!"

Val Douglas came in, strolling leisurely, in order not to joggle the cigarette he was making. He stood on spread legs, and across the cigarette as he licked it shut he looked at the others with an innocent gravity.

"Douglas," Sheriff Amos demanded, "where was you riding last Monday?"

72

"I reckon I was in Nine-Mile Valley," Douglas said.

"How far is that from Slinkard's Hole?"

"About fifteen mile."

"And you and Baker covered both Nine-Mile Valley and Slinkard's Hole in one day?"

Val Douglas was suddenly motionless. He had started to light up, and now his hands stopped with the match half way to his cigarette. Without moving his head he glanced at Dunn, then at Gil Baker, who tried to signal him something by the narrowing of an eye. The match went out, unguarded.

The 94 wagon boss relaxed. "Me and Gil split off, about three miles from the home corrals," he said.

"Yet," said the sheriff, "you never told your boss where you'd been, or why you changed your plans!"

Douglas struck a fresh match. "I'm wagon boss," he said shortly. "When Dunn says count cows, we count cows. But nobody tells me where to ride—they ask me where to ride."

The sheriff stared at him; then he grinned, wholeheartedly, without pretense. "We'll go over to Judge Shafer's office now," he said. "But take my advice. Talk over your story—and try to get together on it!"

He looked like a satisfied mountain lion, full-fed on somebody's top-string colt.

CHAPTER ELEVEN

OUTSIDE, HORSE DUNN TURNED TO BILLY WHEELER. "Guess you better get Marian. This here's the part I want her to see."

Marian was waiting in the side street to which Horse

73

Dunn had sent her with his car; and inevitably, to the grim weariness of Billy Wheeler, Val Douglas was there, helping her wait. Wheeler walked to the door of the car, a tall, narrow-hipped figure, with a deceptively lazy stride.

"We're starting now," he said.

"You run on, Val," Marian said; "I want to talk to Billy."

"Sure, hon." The wagon boss shot Wheeler a glance like a straight left, and went his way, leisurely swaggering.

"I'm kind of glad you sent him on," Wheeler told Marian. "There's one thing I'd kind of like to say." His grey eyes drifted to the horizon beyond the streets. "This hearing—it doesn't amount to much, in a way. If I lose out, the real fight will come in district court, not here. But in another way, I think you're going to see an almighty funny thing, the like of which you maybe never saw before. You're going to see the whole range lined up against one man."

"Against—"

"Against Horse Dunn. It's always this way where there's a free-for-all scrap for range. He's fought fair, and more than fair. But there's more than fifteen outfits in this town right now—and all with the hatchet out for Horse Dunn. Now I want you to watch these men; look at their faces, and their eyes when they watch Horse Dunn. Because maybe it'll help you understand some of the things Horse has to do, sometimes. See?"

"You don't think anything will happen today, do you?"

"I don't think so. Of course if—but I don't look for anything. We better be walking on around to the court, now."

74

"Billy, there's something I want to say, too."

Wheeler looked at her. The blue of her eyes seemed strikingly fresh and cool in the dusty heat. In the moonlight of a mountain trail that he remembered she had seemed a mystery, a white magic not to be believed. But she did not need moonlight to represent a magic. Here in the blasting sun and white dust of the Inspiration street, she seemed more actual, but no less desirable—and unattainable.

"It's just this: I'd give anything in the world if I could testify for you. But I just didn't see it the way—the way it seemed to you."

"I didn't ask you to speak for me," he reminded her.

"Billy, don't! Can't we be friends? Can't we—"

"No," he said.

"But why? Can't you see—"

He turned to look at her, steadily, as he had hardly dared to look at her since his return to the 94; and the blaze of the sun gave her to him an unforgettable clarity of detail—the shadow of her lashes, the blue trace of veins in her temples and forearms, the haze of pure sunlight in her hair. He looked her in the eyes, and said slowly, "If I can't have all of you, then I don't want any of you at all. Do you understand that?"

He thought she colored, very faintly. "Suppose I don't choose to understand that?"

"Then swing wide," he heard himself say. "Swing wide and stay clear! And I shouldn't have to tell you that again."

There was a peculiar gleam in her cool, amazingly clear eyes. "I don't think you're so dangerous," she said.

"I don't know what you mean."

She dropped her voice into a drawl, mocking his own. "I mean—if you and I were left afoot, on some far mountain, at night, all alone with only one blanket between us—I shouldn't be afraid of anything happening, not anything at all."

He turned on her, low-voiced. "Then," he said, "you're a fool." He snapped the car door open.

Marian Dunn hesitated a moment more; then stepped out of the car and walked ahead of him up the street.

Henry Shafer, justice of what peace that was left, was a limited little man, mild and watery of eye. He had spent all his life in this one town, and he had never made any enemies because he had never taken sides. So finally he had got himself elected to office, an honor which he appreciated more greatly than anything that had ever happened to him in his life. Nobody had ever accused him of dishonesty.

His office, in which they now gathered, was an exceedingly small frame structure; three or four wooden steps led up from the sidewalk to the door, and upon the window were painted the words "Real Estate, Insurance, and Justice of the Peace." Inside, in a corner, was a roll-top desk bearing a vast dusty litter, but a long, time-scarred table took up most of the little space. At the head of this sat the paunchy little justice, at his right hand a constable who looked like an elderly cowboy down on his luck.

Horse Dunn—his great size made the room suddenly seem even smaller than it was—shouldered in without greeting to anyone. He shot a contemptuous glance about the walls, which were decorated with a parcel post map, a calendar advertising tick dip, and stains from leaks in the roof; then planted himself facing the door with his back against the wall—an instinctive provision. Shafer jumped up and hustled around the table to place a chair for Marian at the end opposite himself, and when

76

this was done the remainder of the room filled rapidly with sombreroed men.

Link Bender was there, looking hard-bitten and taciturn, and so was Rufe Deane, a green-eyed man with heavy sorrel eyebrows and a storm-carved face; the lanky Pinto Halliday took up an uncomfortable position in the corner by the door. And there were other cattlemen, and some of the cowboys and line riders from the outfits of these men, cramming what little space was left.

Marian was looking the crowd over thoughtfully, but Wheeler could not read her face. To anyone who had lived in the cow country all his life, this scene had elements of the unbelievable. The press of men in this room were Dunn's neighbors, who had known him for years; yet no word was exchanged between these others and the boss of the 94. There was something unnerving in the silence, and the lack of expression in all those desert-weathered faces; you could feel in that room a tireless, long-waiting hostility.

Horse Dunn growled into Wheeler's ear, "Wish Bob Flagg could see this. Anything like this always tickled him."

"I take it this is the case against William Wheeler," said Shafer unnecessarily "Go ahead and open the court."

The constable half rose. His voice was thick, as if he had stagefright—or perhaps the oppressive quiet of that uncommon crowd bore down on him. "She's off," he said, and sat down again.

"Who's prosecuting this case?"

The sheriff said, "I am, Judge. The district attorney's gone up-state to sit in on the Democratic committee, like you know."

"I see here," said Shafer, fussing with papers, "you got him charged with resisting an officer; bearing arms against authority; assault, assault and battery; assault with a deadly weapon, and assault with intent to kill."

"What about assault on horseback?" said Billy Wheeler.

"Never heard of it," said Shafer.

Sheriff Amos looked disgusted. "Let's get on with it."

"William Wheeler, do you plead guilty or not guilty?"

"Not guilty."

"What seems to have gone on here?" Shafer asked Amos.

"Judge," said Walt Amos, "since this ruckus on Short Crick there's been a lot of people trampling around there, gumming up the evidence. So we made deputies of Pinto Halliday and Kid Bender, and we sent 'em to Short Crick to keep fellers out of there. Now yesterday this Wheeler come prowling around there, and when the Kid told him to beat it, he wouldn't go. The Kid tried to argue with him, but this feller got tough, and they had words. The upshot was, Wheeler drew his gun and fired. He—"

Wheeler broke in. "Well, of all the infernal—"

"Keep quiet," said Shafer. The 94 men exchanged glances.

"Well," the sheriff went on, "he didn't hit anything, but the flash of the gun was right under the nose of the Kid's horse, and she rared over backwards on him. The Kid come out of it with concussion of the brain, fracture of the tibia, and two busted ribs."

"Fracture of the what?" said Wheeler.

"It means he busted his arm," Shafer said.

"Leg," Amos corrected.

"That's what I meant," Shafer said. "Is Kid Bender
78

here?"

"Not on a busted leg, Judge. But I got his sworn statement here."

"Now, now! You can't put that in," Wheeler objected. "Either you have to let me cross-examine him, or you can't put in his statement at all."

"Oh, a saddle lawyer, huh?" Amos snarled at him. "I suppose if the guy was dead the case would be closed, according to that!"

"You can't put in any such statement unless it's a dying statement," Wheeler insisted.

"Well, we'll see what it says, anyway," Shafer decided. "Justice is what we're after here!"

Amos now produced and read aloud Kid Bender's statement—a repetition of his own.

"You got any questions, Wheeler?"

Wheeler was appalled. It had not occurred to them that Bender's people would attempt so baldfaced a lie. What had started out as a sample of irritable officiousness had suddenly taken on unknown possibilities. Angering, Wheeler promised himself that once Horse Dunn was extricated he would clean house in this county if it took half of all he had.

"The Kid isn't here to *be* questioned," he snapped.

"I'll call Pinto Halliday," Amos said.

The lanky Halliday came out of a corner reluctantly, looking ill-natured; and a swarthy cowboy who had no official business there was persuaded to give Halliday his seat at the table.

Under the questioning of Walt Amos, Pinto Halliday now stated that he had been in a different part of the Short Creek cuts. Being down in the arroyo, he had not seen the shot fired; but he was riding to join Kid Bender and he had ridden up out of the cut in time to see the

Kid down under his fallen horse, and Billy Wheeler with a smoking gun in his hand.

Billy Wheeler demanded, "You mean to sit there and—"

"You stay in your chute," the judge warned him.

"Pinto," Amos said, "was there anybody else with Wheeler?"

"Miss Dunn, here, was with Wheeler."

"Look here," Wheeler broke in again. "What's the idea dragging her into this?"

"We'll leave her out if you will," Amos said.

"He's got a right to drag in anybody he wants to," Shafer gave his opinion, "so long as it's competent and material. And constitutional."

"Did Miss Dunn say anything?"

"Miss Dunn rides down and jumps off her horse, and she wipes off Kid Bender's face with her handkerchief. And she looks square at this jigger and she says, 'There wasn't no excuse for it,' she says."

Billy Wheeler looked at Marian. The girl sat with her cheek leaned upon one hand; her face was quiet, her eyes sober and watchful.

"That's all," said Amos.

"What's the idea," Shafer asked Wheeler sternly, "pulling a gun on an officer?"

Wheeler ignored him. "Halliday," he said, "how far away were you when you heard the shot fired?"

"I'd say about three hundred yards."

"Yet right away you saw this smoke from my gun— three hundred yards away? That gun sure must have sent up a smudge!"

"By the time I came out of the cut I was closer—not over a hundred yards."

"How long after the shot was that?"

"I'd say about five seconds."

"What'll you take for the horse?"

"Huh?"

"If that horse went two hundred yards and climbed out of a draw in five seconds, he sure must be a streak of light!"

"Well, maybe it was ten or fifteen seconds."

"And what did you say I had smoking in my hand, all this time?"

"A gun, by God!"

"The way you tell it," Wheeler said, "it sounds more like a smoke bomb."

"You trying to make a fool of me?" Pinto demanded.

"Did you notice the Kid's gun was out?"

"I suppose it fell out when his horse went down."

"You mean, you figure his gun fell out of his holster and into his hand—and the fall brought the gun to full cock?"

"I never seen no gun in his hand!" said Pinto stubbornly.

"That's all."

"That's all the witnesses there is to this, Judge Shafer," Amos said. "I can call in the doctor to speak on how bad Kid Bender was hurt, but it don't hardly seem we need him. This is a right simple case, with plenty eye witness. Looks like that ought to be enough."

Shafer looked doubtful. "Well—what you got to say, Wheeler?"

"I plead self defense, Judge," said Wheeler. "Kid Bender made a surprise draw; I grabbed his bit and raised his horse up to make him miss. But it was his own gun going off that made his horse go over. I pulled my gun and stood ready in case he took another shot at me; but I didn't fire, then or any time."

81

"What was the idea resisting an officer in the first place?" Shafer said.

"The only thing I resisted was getting shot."

"Well, call your witnesses."

"I'm not calling any."

Shafer looked surprised; he glanced at Marian Dunn. I thought—"

"I move this case be dismissed," said Wheeler.

"You move *what*?" Shafer demanded. "You know darn well I can't dismiss it! What becomes of this country if—"

"All you've got here is a statement from a little punk who doesn't even appear," Wheeler contended. "He may be raving delirious, for all we know. Pinto Halliday is all snarled up in his own rope. He's contradicted himself twice on the speed of his horse; and on top of that he claims he sat a hundred yards away, and saw a gun still smoking a full quarter minute after it was fired. Isn't that wonderful? Because a modern smokeless cartridge makes no smoke puff in the first place."

"Any cartridge will make smoke," Amos contradicted him.

"Fire off a gun," Wheeler suggested, "and let the judge see this big column of smoke."

Sheriff Amos hesitated, looked questioningly at Shafer, made a half movement toward his holster. Then he stood up, and his eyes drifted to the windows, and the open door. And now they all noticed what a crowd had gathered outside the little building, overflowing the sidewalk, so that the street was full of men. It was a quiet crowd, interested, waiting; and it was made up of men that were lean and darkly tanned, and in the work clothes of the range.

There was worry on the young sheriff's face, as he

studied the crowd in the street. "Excuse me a minute," he said.

"Where you going?"

The sheriff looked sheepish, but stubborn. "I don't figure to take any chances. Everybody on the range is interested in this case; it's a test case, in a way. If I'm going to let off a gun, I figure these people out here better be told what the shooting's for."

There was a threat there; more threat in the sheriff's uneasy precautions than bluster could possibly convey.

The little justice of the peace fidgeted. "There's no sense in firing off guns in here. I've seen guns before."

"Well," said Wheeler, "will you admit that Pinto Halliday couldn't have seen any gunsmoke?"

Shafer glared. "Are you questioning me, sir?"

Wheeler shrugged. "Judge, I made a motion to dismiss."

"Well, your motion is thrown out!"

"This is a mighty serious offense, Judge," Amos said. "The law calls for as high as five years for a thing like this. We got to bind him over to district court, naturally. But what we want is to hold him without bail. We—"

They were at the point of the whole thing, now. If the 94 had a chance, it depended on the activity of Wheeler, who, with his credit and his cow finance connections, might gain time for Horse Dunn. Not the danger of ultimate conviction, but delay on a trumped-up charge was what Wheeler feared.

Horse Dunn snarled in his throat, and there was an instant's silence. Nothing could have shown the force of the man, and the resented power he held, better than that! "Order!" said Judge Shafer, looking startled. "Order in the court!" His command sounded fantastic in that quiet room, for Dunn said nothing.

"This," Amos went on, "is a wealthy man, as folks around here go. And he's lined up with a wealthy outfit. But it's people like him that raise the hell around here, always water-hogging, always roughing the range. We can't hardly get through a season any more without some poor feller gets dry-gulched. One's been killed only just this week. Now if this guy can pull a gun on an officer, and put him out of business, and then walk out of here, free and sassy—then we aren't going to have any law at all, and I can't answer for it. That's all I got to say."

"You want to say anything, Wheeler?" Shafer asked.

"Judge, if it's got so a man can't even put up bail while he waits for a trial in district court, then there's no justice left."

"I'll decide that," Shafer said tartly. "If it's come to a pass where—"

"Now you look here," Horse Dunn boomed.

"Quiet here!" Shafer snapped. "I can't see but what the sheriff's position is reasonable, and more than reasonable. The statement sworn to by Kid Bender and the statement by the defendant is two different things; but there's a witness backing up Kid Bender. There's been altogether too much gun-toting and general ructions on this range. I—"

The mumble of many voices in the street was unobtrusive, and the dense throng of men in that crowded little room had gtood quiet, almost solemn in their Indian-like silence. But now that they foresaw the drift, the quiet began to crumble. The faces of Bender, Rufe Deane, and Halliday remained hard and set, but the cowboys began to grin; and swiftly a murmur rose into a general wordless rumble of encouragement, like a cheer.

84

The effect on Shafer was immediate. His mild eyes shone sternly and he straightened in his chair. "Way I see it—what can American law officers do without the support of the courts of justice?" he asked; and, "Nothing!" he answered himself. "This open flaunting of the law must stop! The very existence of this great state—"

Some kid cowboy sung out, "Pour it into 'em!" and the pack cheered again, grinning. Horse Dunn's eye blazed as if he bad been slapped across the face. Wheeler set his jaw. "Hold steady," he said to Horse Dunn. "For God's sake, sit tight!" The boss of the 94 did not seem to hear him.

Shafer inflated. "We are here today—" he went on, his voice rising.

"Just a minute," Marian Dunn said.

Judge Shafer halted in full career; and abruptly a new motionless silence came over the people packed into that room, at the sound of the girl's voice. "Heh?" said Shafer.

"I'll testify."

For a moment Shafer seemed not to comprehend, and there was a moment more of that dense heavy quiet.

Sheriff Walt Amos spoke, his voice flat, ironic, and his contempt for the judge was in it—the contempt of a quick-thinking man for a slow one. "She can't testify."

"Why can't she?"

"Because she hasn't been called by either side."

"I want you people to know," said Judge Shafer, "that I'm running this court!"

In the heavy quiet while Shafer still hesitated, Wheeler watched the faces of Horse Dunn's enemies. The young cowboys were unwillingly friendly to the girl, swayed by an inevitable attraction. But in the faces

85

of the cow bosses Wheeler saw a strange thing. These older, embittered men were seeing Marian not as a girl but as a part of the 94. He noticed the dark, hard gaze of Link Bender, and the unforgettable green eyes of Rufe Deane, the man who blamed Dunn for the death of his son. There was no more compromise in these men than in the edge of an obsidian knife; and to them the girl was a sexless enemy.

"This court means to serve out right and justice, not technicalities," Shafer decided. "And if Miss Dunn wants to testify, I'll call her as a witness for the court."

There was a moment's pause. "I was at Short Creek," Marian said.

"Go ahead, Miss Dunn—just tell the court what you saw, in your own words."

Marian Dunn still sat with her cheek rested upon her hand; her eyes flicked to Horse Dunn, then to Billy Wheeler, but conveyed nothing. "I was only a little distance away—I saw all of it. Kid Bender rode up out of the bed of the creek, running his horse so hard he had to slide it to keep from knocking Wheeler's horse over. They sat there talking; Kid Bender seemed to be threatening Wheeler. Finally—"

"Now why do you say 'seem'?" Walt Amos broke in. "Either you heard what was said or you didn't."

"Let her tell her story!"

"Finally," Marian continued, "Kid Bender motioned with his head toward where I was sitting, and Billy Wheeler turned, as if to see where I was. While Billy Wheeler was turned away Kid Bender jerked out his gun. It was the most unfair, unwarranted thing you could possibly imagine."

"You mean to say—"

"Be still!" said Shafer.

"Wheeler saw the gun just in time. He half dropped out of the saddle—evidently trying to avoid the shot; he seemed to try to get the neck of Bender's horse between himself and the gun. Just then Bender's gun went off. Both horses jumped; but Bender's reared, and fell over backwards."

"Well, when did Wheeler fire?"

"He didn't fire at all."

"But what about this gunsmoke?"

"I didn't see any smoke. There was a lot of dust going up from the ground, but that was all."

"This is remarkable," said Shafer.

"It's an almighty funny thing," Amos said, "that this wasn't put in by the defendant in the first place!"

"You want to cross-examine, Amos?"

"I certainly do," said the sheriff. "Look here, Miss Dunn! How long have you known this man Wheeler?"

"What's the point to that?" Wheeler demanded.

"Judge," said Amos, "I claim this woman is—"

"Watch yourself!" said Billy Wheeler.

There was a general stir through all that dense press of men. "Come to order!" said Shafer. I—"

"I don't mean," Billy Wheeler began, "to let this—"

"Will you come to order," said Shafer, "or take a contempt of court?"

Outside there now rose a new disturbance as a dust-crusted car came careening down the street; it half spun as it skidded to a stop in the middle of the roadway in front of Shafer's office. Sam Caldwell, square-set, heavy-necked ally of Link Bender, forged his way through the crowd and came shouldering up the steps. Inside and outside the quiet broke into mumbling disorder.

"You want me to finish with cross-questioning this

87

witness," the sheriff was demanding of the judge, "or not? If you want me to clear this court—"

"I've never had to clear a court yet," said Shafer. "I—what's going on here?"

He sat back and stared scowling at the disturbance which set the whole room in motion as Sam Caldwell thrust his way through the door and up to the table. Reaching it, Caldwell jerked off his big hat, and threw it on the table like an oldtime fighter throwing his hat into the ring. His face was steaming red, heavily marked with dust-muddied sweat.

"I got to speak to the sheriff a minute," he said.

Sheriff Walt Amos struggled to get to his feet in the close press. "Alone?" he asked Caldwell.

Judge Shafer flared up. "This is a court of law and I mean to have it treated as such. A hearing is going on here for a serious offense. You can't come in here and—"

Caldwell looked at Judge Shafer heavily, with the dislike that hard-riding cattlemen have for men whom they consider ineffectual. "This might still be more interesting around here than that," he said. "There's a man been killed—another, by God!—cut in two with a shotgun at Ace Springs."

There was a second or two in which the throng was silent with the sudden struck silence of animals at the report of a gun, before there arose the inevitable buzz and stir. Ace Springs was 94 water.

Walt Amos said sharply, "Sam, who's killed?"

"Cayuse Cayetano! Dead since yesterday."

CHAPTER TWELVE

As word of Cayuse Cayetano's murder swept through the street, the loosely grouped crowd shifted and seemed to seethe, gathering in knots. The half-breed tracker had been loved by none, respected by none; but his trail genius was undisputed, and it had been widely rumored that he was very close to important revelations. Half a dozen men tried to follow Sam Caldwell into the already crowded county office, forcing in through a considerable number of the crowd inside who had immediately started to make their way out.

Though it was Judge Shafer's boast that he had never had to clear a court in his life, he was induced to do so now. He glanced about him, looking for something to pound with; he found nothing, and stood up. "Clear them out of here! Clear the court of everybody that doesn't belong here! By God, I'll finish trying this case if it's the last thing I do!"

"Everybody out!" the sheriff shouted at them. "Outside, all of you! Will you move or not?"

The packed crowd within the close four walls began to move reluctantly, each one of those independent men having to make sure separately that the order was really intended for himself. If it did not take long to clear that court it was because the room was small.

"You, Sam," the sheriff ordered, "you wait here. No—go out and get my deputies back in here. Where's Rufe Deane—Link Bender? Tell 'em I want 'em here. By God, here's just one more sample of what I was telling you! Cayuse was close to naming the Short Crick murderer. Judge, the range won't stand it!"

"If you've got your court clear, let's have order," said Judge Shafer. "I mean to get this over with. Wheeler, is your defense finished?"

"You yourself called the only eye witness here, and the only witness worth a whoop," Wheeler said. "That ought to be defense enough for any man."

"You got anything more to say, sheriff?"

"Get it over with," snapped the sheriff. "If you're going to let in testimony like that last, I can't stop you. And I've got other work to do."

"This is as unsatisfactory a case as I've ever seen on this bench," Judge Shafer said. "Something's wrong— something's very wrong. I'd like to reserve decision and think it over."

"Reserve, hell! Let's have it, one way or the other," Amos demanded.

"All right! All right! Have it your own way! Case dismissed!"

Sheriff Walt Amos angrily crashed his open hand upon the table top and stood up. "There's a sweet decision!"

"Any other court would give you a contempt for that," said Shafer waspishly. "Lock up the place, Harry. The court stands adjourned!"

He crammed his papers into his brief case and stalked out, looking angry, insulted, and anxious to get away from there. Nobody spoke to him or interfered with him as he went down the steps and out of sight in the street, moving at a hurried amble.

Sam Caldwell came back in, bringing with him Pinto Halliday and Link Bender, their deputies' badges half hidden, but evident.

"You want me?" said Link.

"Stick around here. Where's Rufe Deane?"

"He'll be here in a minute."

"There's other work to do," said Link Bender, "that can't be done here. I better be getting at it!"

"Stay here," said Walt Amos shortly.

Link Bender stared at him a moment, then leaned against the wall, his dark hawk face hard and tightlipped.

"If you're through with us we'll be leaving," said Horse Dunn.

"I'm not through with you. I'll tell you when I'm through."

"You'll have to let my wagon boss go, so's he can drive my niece back to the ranch," Horse Dunn told him.

The sheriff looked at Dunn for a moment, without seeming to see him, he appeared to be listening, or weighing other things. "All right. On condition that he immediately gets out of town. An hour from now I don't want to find he's still here."

"I'll be out of here, all right," Val Douglas said.

"Well, I'll see you start. You ready, Miss Dunn?"

"Better take my roadster Marian," Billy Wheeler said. He gave her the key, and she accepted it without meeting his eyes.

"You boys," the sheriff said to the deputies, "keep the 94 outfit handy." He followed Val Douglas and Marian Dunn into the street.

When they were gone an oppressive quiet descended upon the room. With only the 94 men and the deputies in it, the room somehow seemed smaller than before, holding the opposed parties together to the distaste of both. Sam Caldwell turned his broad back squarely upon the 94 men and consulted in undertones with Link Bender and Pinto Halliday in the corner by the door.

Five minutes passed.

Horse Dunn motioned his men close to him. "Keep together," he said. "And don't let nobody get you loose from your guns."

Sheriff Walt Amos came back in.

"Dunn," he said at once, "where was Val Douglas yesterday?"

"He was in Nine-Mile Valley," Dunn said.

"And that's not so far from Ace Springs, is it?"

"Not so far."

"But riding toward Santiam he'd be going just the opposite way from Ace Springs, wouldn't he?"

"What's that got to do with it?"

"Toward Santiam," said the sheriff, "was where he said he was, just this minute when I asked him. What's your answer to that?"

The two men eyed each other. "If he said he was up toward Santiam, he was probably up toward Santiam," Dunn said.

The sheriff grunted and half grinned, without humor. "How lucky. With a man dead at Ace Springs, naturally Douglas was as far away as he could get! Where were you, Wheeler?"

One by one they each gave their answers, tersely, without conciliation, as the same question was put to each.

"I want you boys," the sheriff said to his deputies, "to remember what these men have said."

"You figure to keep us here all night?" Horse Dunn demanded.

"I'm going to turn you out of here in ten minutes," Amos said.

Rufe Deane, swinging up the wooden steps, was in time to catch sheriff's answer. He now thrust in, his green eyes ugly under his shaggy sorrel brows. "You're going to what?" he said.

"I have no intention," the sheriff said, "of holding these men on what we got against 'em so far."

Rufe Deane angered with an obvious, unexpected violence. "You mean to stand there and tell me you're going to cut 'em loose?"

"I mean I'll take who I want to, and when I want to, and I won't be told different by my deputies or anybody else!"

"By God, Walt," said Link Bender, "Rufe's right. You can't—"

"Keep quiet," Amos snapped at him. Link Bender's eyes narrowed but he shut his mouth.

"These men'll never leave this town," said Rufe Deane.

"I decide that here," said the sheriff.

Rufe Deane stared at him a moment longer, green fury in his eyes. Suddenly he tore off his deputy's badge and threw it on the floor. "Maybe you do," he said. He turned and went out into the street, the high heels of his boots clumping slowly, restrained; but as he disappeared from view they heard his step quicken on the board walk.

Walt Amos said, "You want that badge, Sam?"

Sam Caldwell hesitated a moment. "All right," he said.

The sheriff turned on his remaining deputies. "If either of you want to string with Rufe Deane, now's the time to say so! Because the next job of this office is to guarantee these men safe conduct out of town."

"Walt," said Link Bender, "I'm for you and I always have been; and there's mighty few jobs I'd back off from as a peace officer. But I don't know as I can bring

93

myself to turn my hand to that!"

Horse Dunn spoke up, his voice rumbling in his chest. "Who the hell wants safe conduct?" he said contemptuously. "When you're tired of jawing, we'll move on out."

Walt Amos turned his back on them, and stood staring out into the sun-blasted street. That street was curiously empty—unwholesomely empty, so that nobody who had seen the crowd there could look at that street now without knowing that something was irregular, something wrong.

"Move out, then," the sheriff said. "Drag your freight and drag it quick. Keep going. Five minutes from now I don't want you in this town."

Horse Dunn chuckled in his short beard and hitched his belt up. Slowly he sauntered past the deputies, staring at each of them with an open insolent amusement as he passed; then he shouldered out, a huge hulk that filled the whole frame of the door.

Unhurrying, the 94 men made their way along the main street of Inspiration, around the corner to their car. Unquestionably it had been Rufe Deane's intention that the 94 men should never leave that town. Sullen groups that loitered about doorways silently watched them pass. Certain cowboy hangouts—the feed barn, the saddlery, the blacksmith shop—were full of men. But in the open sunlight of midday, Rufe Deane and his supporters were caught short of time, and nobody attempted to bar Horse Dunn's way.

But as the dust of Inspiration kicked out from under their tires they knew that they had put behind them a violence that was not avoided, but only delayed.

CHAPTER THIRTEEN

By the time they reached the ranch it was already late afternoon, and the tall Tuscaroras were sending vast, vague fingers of shadow about the layout of the 94, while the high eastern horizon was still brightly brassy in the sun. Marian did not come out to meet them. Hunting around, Horse Dunn presently sighted her sitting on the fence of a little empty corral, hidden from the house by the barns. He walked out to climb the fence beside her; and Billy Wheeler, tired of people around him, went to his room, and got his razors out.

Here Horse presently came looking for him. The old cow boss walked in slowly, and closed the door after him. He sat down on the edge of the bunk with the movements of a man a hundred years old; and he covered his face with his hands.

"You know what she said to me?" he demanded.

"Nope."

"I went out to where she's sitting on that corral. I just wanted to tell her about Rufe Deane throwing down his deputy badge, and the way they cleared the street. I thought maybe if she's seen it all she'd know what we're up against. So I went out there and I said, 'Marian—' That was all I said. She never even looked at me. And pretty soon she says—'*You're making this country run red.*'"

Billy Wheeler laid his razor down. "She said that to you?"

" 'You're making this country run red,' " Horse Dunn repeated. "So long as I live, I'll never forget the way she said that."

Suddenly Billy Wheeler felt a detached pity for this old man and this girl. He was able to see what Horse Dunn could not: that the girl was curiously dependent upon this old man, who looked like her father; was dependent upon him in more ways than she was aware. And both were deeply hurt, at a loss, because they could not understand each other.

He could not see much chance that the girl would learn to understand either Horse Dunn or the dry country men whom he faced. Horse Dunn was what the dry country had made him; and there was no longer anything in the old man's life except the cow kingdom he had dreamed, and tried to build, for her.

Horse Dunn straightened up, slapping his knees, and some of the stiffening came back into him. "But that isn't what I come in here to make mention of," he said. "Look here. I didn't want to say anything about this in front of them others. But take a look at that envelope."

The envelope he handed Billy Wheeler was empty, torn across the end. It bore the return address of a cattle loan company two hundred miles away. But on turning it over again something else caught his eye—a peculiarity in the gluing of the flap.

"This thing was steamed open," he said after a moment.

Horse Dunn nodded. "Now you know why the Link Bender crowd is able to time things so good," he said.

"But look here—somebody can be made to sweat for this!"

"What's the good of making some two-for-a-nickel postmaster sweat? The thing is, they've got a line on my business through my mail. By now they know more about it than I do, for all I know!"

"Have they learned anything much?"

"They learned a-plenty, just in that one letter. I've got thirty-eight thousand dollars coming due next week, with that company alone. I wrote them asking for more time. I don't get it. I've got to go there."

"Well, there's sure some way for you to get there—in spite of Amos."

"Sure, I can get there. But what's the good? All the Link Bender crowd has to do is clamp down with their infernal silly murder charge. Who's going to lend money to a cowman under a charge of murder? They'll blow the 94 higher than a kite in a matter of days."

"Horse," said Wheeler with conviction, "one thing's certain. We've got to find Bob Flagg."

Horse Dunn flared up. "And how are we going to find him? He checked out of his hotel at Flagstaff—and where is he now? If it was anybody but Flagg I'd think he'd cut out with the pot. But this is the same damn way he's been all his life! He never lets a man know anything about anything."

"Good heavens, Horse! There must be ways to—"

"Name two," Horse Dunn said morosely. "Well—get Old Man Coffee in here."

Billy Wheeler went out, wiping the lather from his face, and brought Old Man Coffee in. He was not hard to find; in case of doubt he could always be traced in relation to the mournful singing of his dogs. Coffee came in gloomily and threw his coiled dog whip on the floor.

"I havn't actually hit a dog with that thing for over nine days," he offered. "But I swear I come close to hitting one tonight. That old fool makes me so cussed—"

"Coffee," Dunn interrupted, "you haven't been here long; but you've trailed and back-trailed, and promoted all over this place with those long-eared hounds. Now tell me one thing: do you see any show of finding out who killed Lon Magoon?"

Old Man Coffee dropped into a chair and considered for several long moments. "No," he said at last.

"Why?" Dunn demanded.

"Somebody, some place, may have killed Lon Magoon, for all I know. But he sure wasn't killed at Short Crick."

For once in his life old Horse Dunn's jaw dropped. "Look here! You wouldn't go to fooling with me?"

"I don't always know what I'm talking about. This time I know."

"But the saddle—"

"I don't question it was Magoon's saddle; I only say it was a different man was killed in it."

Again Horse stared at Coffee; then he relaxed a little, and sat down on the bunk. "Coffee," he said, "if you're so dead sure, in God's name tell us what you know!"

Coffee squinted his deep-set eyes at Dunn. "I sore-footed a good dog, and like to killed a mule, getting over here to help you with this case. I don't ask for that to be appreciated. But I'm getting a little tired of answering all the questions around here!"

Horse looked baffled. "What's the matter with you?"

"I'm tired of being lied to, for one thing."

"Who's lied to you?"

"More than one, right here on this place. Dunn, there's too many things not open to the eye around here to suit me!"

"Coffee," said Horse Dunn without belligerence, "what in all hell do you mean by that?"

"I'll just give you one sample." Old Man Coffee picked up his dog whip from the floor and sorted out its coils with bony old fingers. "There's been a horse in

98

this case that's been known as the killer's horse, because he left his trail at Short Crick, mixed up in the sign of the killing. You know I took old Rock and we trailed that horse; though it come to nothing, then. Now, since we've been back here this afternoon, I've seen a funny thing. Rock's been working around the horse corrals, by himself; trying to work out a trail. Dog voices is peculiar—they call different trails in different ways. And as soon as I heard Rock's voice, I knew he was crying the trail of the killer horse."

They stared at him in silence. Then Horse Dunn said, "You're telling me that the killer's horse has been here in this layout—right here—within the past few days?"

"Within the past twenty-four hours," Coffee said.

Horse Dunn made a gesture of impatience, almost of disgust "I swear I never heard the beat," he said. "You set out to give me a sample of how you've been done wrong by, around here. And what does it come to? You read names, dates and places into the howl of a hound; and you figure out that right here among us he's come on a trail that he completely lost when he had the straight run of it."

"You asked me for a sample of something peculiar around here," Old Man Coffee said. "I give it you."

"Well, why in all hell," Dunn demanded, "didn't you take the hound and trace out where the suspicious horse track went?"

"That's what made me sore at old Rock," Coffee said. "As soon as I went near him he quit cold. He remembered that combing over I gave him yesterday, on that same trail, 1 guess. And now he's under the bunk house, be damned if he'll come out."

"All right. What's some other sample?"

"I've no mind to argue with you," said Coffee.

Horse Dunn's voice hardened a shade. "There's just one little point you made, Coffee, where I think we've got an argument coming. A minute ago you said you'd been lied to here. Now I want to know how you back that up."

"You want me to back that up?" Coffee appeared to consider. "It's pretty near time to eat," he said finally. "I'll back that one statement I made—that one and no more—after we've et."

" 'After we've et,' " Dunn repeated. "You figure that gorging yourself is more important than thrashing out this case ?"

"Yes," said Old Man Coffee.

Horse Dunn threw up his hands and went stalking out.

"Seems like you always set out to rile him," Wheeler accused Coffee.

"Yes, and maybe he riles me some!" Old Man Coffee made his long dog whip writhe in lazy figure eights upon the floor; then, sighting a fly upon the screen, he let the long lash drift the length of the room. It popped like a firecracker, and the fly was not in existence any more. Coffee smiled faintly in approval. "Sometimes you might's well meet a thing a-coming, son."

CHAPTER FOURTEEN

THE MOUNTAINS WERE THROWING THEIR EARLY LUCID twilight across the range of the 94 by the time the cowboys cleared their supper plates. They had eaten in silence. But somehow in the interval since the conference in Billy Wheeler's room, everybody there had learned about the quarrel that was smoking up between Old Man Coffee and Horse Dunn. So now they still loafed in the mess shack, and nobody spoke of seven-up. They rolled cigarettes and lighted pipes, and a couple of lamps were lit, throwing tall, huge shadows of the men on the walls behind. They all knew that the 94 was up against a thrash-out, within itself.

"I hear," Val Douglas said to Old Man Coffee, "you've got a talking dog."

"News travels," said Old Man Coffee.

"I hear your dog says that the killer's horse has been in this layout within the past two days."

"So he tells me."

"Coffee," said Douglas, "that's my idea of a very doggone peculiar thing; maybe just a little too peculiar to rest on the hollering of a hound."

"I've noticed more than one peculiar thing," Old Man Coffee said.

"I've noticed one or two myself," Douglas said, eyeing him. "For one thing, this is getting to be an uncommonly hard place to sleep at night, what with fellers getting up out of their bunks and prowling all over the spread."

"You want to know who walks around here at night?" Coffee said. "I walk around here at night."

"Learn anything?" said Douglas sarcastically.

Old Man Coffee's eyes snapped down out of pipe smoke to meet those of Douglas. "Maybe I have," he said.

Wheeler looked over the tall wagon boss, and he knew more than ever that he didn't like this man. "I wouldn't put up my back if I was you," he said to Douglas. "What little has been found out about this case has been found out by Old Man Coffee; and God knows it's been through no help from you!"

"What do you mean by that?"

"Twice you told us you were going one place and you went a different place. The sheriff is an inexperienced kid, but he ran *you* up a tree—and made fools of us all."

"If I didn't tell you where I went," Douglas said hotly, "it was because it didn't come up."

"There's all ways of bending the truth," said Coffee.

Billy Wheeler said, "I'm beginning to ask myself who around here is afraid of the truth!"

Marian Dunn spoke, her voice husky and very low. In that room were Gil Baker, Steve Hurley, Tulare Callahan, Horse Dunn; and the ancient Tia Cara was just beyond the door. But now as Marian spoke it was as if she were alone with just Billy Wheeler and Val Douglas, and none of the others counted at all. "I'll say this," she said. "I'd believe Val Douglas more quickly than I'd believe myself."

Billy Wheeler was silent. He know that she felt she had sworn to a false statement—in his behalf; and that she could not forgive him for that. But her evidence had not been only truth; it had offered the only hope of arriving at either truth or justice. He thought her attitude was completely unreasonable. If he could only make her see—

Horse Dunn broke the silence impatiently. "There sure ought to be enough scrapping on this range without hunting up trouble among ourselves. In ordinary times this whole killing case wouldn't amount to a tinker's damn to begin with."

"I'm not so sure," said Old Man Coffee.

"What kind of a case have they got?" Horse demanded. "They can't even find their everlasting stiff!"

"They're pretty liable to find it," Old Man Coffee

102

thought. "When they find it, it'll be about all they need. If it's Magoon, like you claim, they can show motive—you said openly that you'd kill Magoon if you caught him on 94 range. They've got opportunity—by your own statement you were riding alone on Red Sleep Ridge that day, and the Red Sleep is within striking distance of Short Crick. They can prove you hid the dead man's saddle—which they can stretch to make look like a concealment of the crime. And all this says nothing about the killing of Cayuse Cayetano."

"What's known about the killing of Cayuse?"

"How do I know? We're so popular around here we can't even go look over Ace Springs without getting into a scrap with officers of the peace—same as Billy got into at Short Crick."

Dunn slumped down in his chair and went to growling into his war-like beard. "I don't believe you know any more about it than the rest of us do."

"I'll put it stronger than that. Maybe—" Old Man Coffee made each word separately heard—"someone in this room knows a whole lot more than I know!"

Horse Dunn sat perfectly still, except for his eyes; his head did not raise and no muscle of his face changed, but his eyes whipped to the old lion hunter's face. After a moment he said, "Coffee, that's one remark you're sure going to have to back up."

"I'll say just one thing more. There's scarcely a man in this room that hasn't lied to me at least once, in the little time I've been here."

Horse Dunn sat up slowly, hitching himself square in this chair. "Maybe some of my boys have been a little hazy and loose-spoken about where they've been, and when. No man knows what he's up against here. Take Gil, here—the sheriff mixed him up. And why? Because

103

Gil would try to stand by his side riders even if he knew every last one of 'em was guilty. If you hold that against him, then maybe you know dogs—but you're nuts!"

Old Man Coffee spoke past the pipe stem in his teeth. "I suppose that lets you out, too?" He sat looking at Dunn steadily, a little smile on his face.

Horse spread his hands in front of him on the table, as if he would jump across it, and his voice rose like the voice of a bull. "If you say I lied, then by God name what you mean!"

"To hell with you," Coffee said, without lifting his voice.

"You'll either back what you said," the outraged Horse Dunn stormed, "or you'll swaller it whole!"

"That I won't do either," Coffee said.

For a moment Horse Dunn stared at him blankly; then he sat down, and the flame went out of his eyes, giving place to something ugly. "I can't stand for that, Coffee," he said. "You know I can't stand for that."

"I can't help that."

"You don't give me any choice," said Horse Dunn thickly. "You sure you want to stick to what you said?"

"Naturally."

"If you don't want to work with me—I've got along all right so far, and I guess I'll be able to go on struggling along. I—"

"Wait," Billy began. "You—"

"Shut up, Wheeler," Coffee said.

"You've acted like you've wanted out of this ever since I go you in it," Dunn clipped out. "All right then—you're out! And you can send me a bill for what I owe."

Old Man Coffee stood up and stretched himself, a queer smile on his face. "Just send me a check for a million dollars," he said. He sauntered out into the dark.

For a few moments after Old Man Coffee had gone out, the 94 people sat silent, unable to realize that the old lion hunter was no longer of their number. From beyond in the young night came the blooping of his hounds; they would go and do their blooping elsewhere, now. Billy Wheeler was thinking that it was a sad thing, but perhaps an inevitable one, that these two old men could not have worked together.

"There goes a queer genius," Tulare Callahan said.

Horse Dunn roused himself. "I always heard he was cranky. But now he's gone cracked altogether. I suppose the old fool won't even stay the night—he'll go sleep in the brush somewhere. Well, fair enough! Somebody go catch his mule."

Two or three of them moved, but Billy Wheeler wanted the job, and he took it. He held a lantern while Coffee saddled his black mule. He knew it was useless to try to get the two old men together again, but he felt that it was one of those things that a man has to try. He kept trying to think of an angle of approach, but Old Man Coffee, whose packing was easily done, was ready to move out before Wheeler thought of a way.

Old Man Coffee extended his hand. "Well, so long, son."

"Mr. Coffee," Wheeler said, "Horse Dunn mighty often doesn't mean what he says; he shouts and hollers, but he's the best-hearted man in the world. I'm mighty sorry to see you bust up with him."

"He doesn't mean what he says, huh?" Old Man Coffee chuckled. "Well, you can tell him that I mean what I say, pretty near every shot!"

"I'm almighty sorry," Wheeler said, "to see you leave this case. You're needed here, if ever a man was."

"Tough," said Old Man Coffee. He swung aboard the black mule and sat looking down at Billy Wheeler from the saddle. "I kind of like you, son. You seem to have a little more savvy than the others. So here's something for you to keep under your hat. I'm not out of this case yet. I'm going to do one more job before I go. I'm going to find the murdered man."

"You think you can?"

"Looks like I might. Horse Dunn—he ain't in on this. He made a fool of me, and himself, too, when he got bullheaded and held onto Magoon's saddle. I told him to turn it in to the sheriff—but no, he had to have his own way. This time I'm running no chances. If I find the dead man, my next move will be to take word to the sheriff."

"And then—"

"And then I'm going off in the brush and sleep for a week."

"But look here! Do you realize, if you do that the Inspiration crowd will be holding every card in the deck? Where does the 94 come in?"

"That's your worry. But I'll help you this much: you be up on Lost Whiskey Butte tomorrow about an hour after sun-up. Tomorrow's going to be my last day's work on this case—I hope. And we'll see what we'll see."

"I'll be there," Wheeler said.

"And don't you bring Horse Dunn—or any of his hired men either. Or by golly, I'll—"

"Okay."

"And meanwhile—if Horse Dunn or any other brush-faced old pelican wants anything from me, you just tell him to go plumb square to hell!" He raised his hat ironically toward the lighted mess shack, and jogged off

106

into the dark, his seven dogs cruising ahead.

When he was gone Billy Wheeler climbed to the top rail of the corral, where he sat despondently eyeing the horizon stars. For the first time he felt an overwhelming sense of the 94's helplessness against odds. Everything had gone against Horse Dunn; the outfit was confused, disorganized, at a loss. He had no desire to go back to the others. He sat where he was until presently the lights in the mess shack were blown out, and figures moved away from the door. He saw lights come on in the ranch house and in the bunk house. Far out across the flats he heard the bloop of old Rock.

He was trying to account for the vague claims of the old lion hunter: Coffee's opinion that there had been a third man at the Short Creek killing; that the so-called killer's horse had been in the 94 layout within the past twenty-four hours; that Lon Magoon was alive—or at least had not been killed at Short Creek; his accusation, obviously astounding to Horse Dunn himself, that Horse Dunn had lied.

And behind these things in his mind was one question that now stood out more largely than them all. Where was Bob Flagg? To Billy Wheeler it seemed that the appearance of Bob Flagg, and this alone, could give them any chance to extricate the 94 from the trap it was in.

Marian Dunn, he noticed, still stood talking to Val Douglas, lingering outside the door of the ranch house. In the stillness of the night he could hear the low continuous murmur of Val's voice, talking steadily—doubtless in his own behalf. And he could see Marian's lowered profile against the yellow light of a window pane. It was curious how every suggested line of that girl, every least bend of her head could move Billy

Wheeler, twist him inside. Resolutely he set his mind upon Bob Flagg—the key to the situation, the man whose appearance, if only he could be found, would give them a breathing spell, and a fighting chance.

What happened then was a strange thing—strange in that Billy Wheeler had almost a forenotice of it. As he sat there alone in the dark he now found himself keenly aware of the peopled layout about him—aware of the exact location of the men in the bunk house! of the ponies in the corrals. It was a peculiar sensation, as if he were suddenly more awake than before, as awake as a man in a ring battle, or a man in danger.

And especially he was aware of the dark, silent brush country at his back, where buckbrush and desert juniper stood thick behind the corrals. Somewhere out there a twig cracked, and his nerves jerked. Something in that black mile of brush was as awake as he.

He swore at himself, trying to forget the profile of Marian Dunn, who stood talking in low murmurs to that tall, too-good-looking wagon boss; trying to forget his sense that the empty brush behind him was no longer empty.

Then abruptly the silence broke, definitely, once-and-for-all, as if the night's shell of stillness had cracked.

Behind Marian's shadowed silhouette the window glass itself shattered, as if it had exploded inward; out in the brush sounded the ringing crack of a rifle. Then there was silence and the window against which Marian had stood was empty except for the lamp-lit gleam of its shattered glass.

Wheeler's breath jerked in his throat; he dropped to the ground and raced for the house.

In the dark beside the shattered window Douglas was holding the girl in his arms, and though she clung to him, Wheeler saw that the wagon boss was holding her up. He heard Douglas say, "Are you hurt? Are you—"

Billy Wheeler cried out, "In God's name, Marian—"

Marian's voice said shakily, "I'm all right."

"You hit?"

"No."

"Get a gun!" said Val Douglas crazily. "We was standing here, and somebody took a shot at—"

Wheeler turned and ran for the bunk house. Half way he almost crashed into Tulare Callahan. "What's up?"

"Get the boys out," Wheeler told him. "To hell with saddles, but get ropes and guns. Somebody fired into the layout—we've got to try to stampede over him in the brush."

It is not easy to make good time roping milling horses in the dark. To Wheeler it seemed a long time, filled with fumbling and cursing and the smashing about of night-frightened horses, before Gil, Steve, and Tulare started with him into the brush behind the 94 layout, mounted bareback on nervous ponies.

CHAPTER FIFTEEN

BEHIND THE 94 LAYOUT THE BUCKBRUSH STOOD ragged, much of it shoulder high to a mounted man; in its crooked brakes the hard sandy ground showed barren in the light of the near stars. Two or three times in the history of the brand the 94 had burned off that brush, but it was hardly worth it, considering the lack of grass roots, and the brush had always come back. A smart horse could sometimes hide himself in that brush in broad daylight. There was practically no chance at all of finding a man there at night.

With some difficulty Billy Wheeler restrained Gil Baker and Steve Hurley from spurring their ponies headlong into the brush, as if they were trying to jump a bunch of steers.

"Stick together, move slow, and keep stopping to listen," Wheeler said. "That's our only chance."

Tulare Callahan thought it would be better to fan out, covering as much ground as possible as quickly as they could. But Wheeler saw the disadvantages in this. "That way no man can count on anything he hears," he said. "We'll be cracking down on each other next."

They trailed into the brush slowly, single file, Wheeler in the lead. He had accidently mounted a horse that believed in ghosts, and it moved side-long, stretching its nose warily at the brush shadows, blowing long uneasy whoofs. Repeatedly they halted to sit listening. It was a silent windless night, but because the brush country has a hidden population that moves at night, they were led this way and that by faint stirrings, distant scratching of twigs.

"If anything moves," Wheeler said, "fire and ride it down."

Perhaps it occurred to none of them that a rider who fired upon a prowling man in that brush would himself be an unmissable mark against the sky, but other things made that hunt an eerie one. A low word would carry a long way in that echoless space. In their certain knowledge that someone was in that brush—probably very close at hand—they knew that they were heard without hearing, seen without seeing. For an hour they combed the dark brush, alternately walking their horses and listening.

Not until they came out at the foot of a barren rise did they realize that they had wandered almost a mile from their starting point. When you have seen one thicket of buckbrush by starlight you have seen them all. They had pushed through a hundred thickets, in which a man could have hidden under the very feet of their horses— yet in that mile of country there were a thousand thickets more. The riders were grim and tight-mouthed. To shoot from cover into a man's layout by night is an intolerable outrage, not to be borne; but they were helpless.

"We should've worked closer to the house," Tulare thought.

"What's the good of that? Give me two minutes' start in this country and you'd never see me again."

"We might's well go on back."

Horse Dunn met them at the corrals. He had been prowling all over the place, rifle on his arm. He spoke low-voiced, but no one of them would have crossed him then, any more than they would have fooled with a fourteen-hand silvertip. His words came out as hard as pieces of rock.

"Go on and turn in," he told them. "This is most likely all for tonight."

"Where's Val Douglas?"

"I told him to stay with Marian."

Naturally, Billy Wheeler thought, Val Douglas would be with Marian—yes, of course, always.

As they went into the house Wheeler saw that Marian had taken up the glass from the shot-smashed window and fitted a cardboard into the broken pane to keep out the blow of the sand.

Horse Dunn said, "Go on and turn in, Val."

When the wagon boss was gone Marian still stood waiting, watching her uncle. Her eyes were bright, and it seemed to Wheeler that there was more color in her

111

face than usual.

"I suppose," Horse Dunn said to her bleakly, "you'll be packing up to be going back home."

"Home? Back east?"

"Naturally. I wouldn't expect you to be staying here. I'm sorry you found your outfit in such bum shape. But it couldn't be helped, I guess."

"But I'm not leaving," Marian said.

"Huh?" said Dunn. "You're not leaving?"

"Of course not."

Horse Dunn stared at her. "I'd sure like to know," he said at last, "just what you think of this—this thing that happened tonight."

"I think western marksmanship has been greatly overrated." They looked at each other for a moment; then Marian smiled, apparently entertained by the blank dumbfoundment on Horse Dunn's face. "I'm going to bed," she announced. At the door she turned and grinned at them both. "Don't worry about it so much," she said.

When she was gone Horse Dunn turned to Billy Wheeler, very much at a loss. "Now who the devil would have thought—"

"You got to pack her out of here," said Billy Wheeler.

"That's up to her," Horse Dunn said.

"Up to her, hell!" said Wheeler. "This is no place for her, and you know it."

Dunn shook his head. "We'll lick this. If she stays here she'll see it all straighten out. But if she leaves here now she'll never come back."

"But damnation, man, it isn't safe for her here! The shot that took out that window couldn't have missed her six inches."

"You know no man in the world would shoot to hit

her! The bushwacker most likely just saw somebody against a window, and took a chance, hopeful it was me. They couldn't make that mistake twice in a thousand years. Ain't enough resemblance, what with the whiskers."

Wheeler saw that the old fighter still could not face a withdrawal of the girl from his life. "Next," he said with disgust, "you'll have 'em shooting apples off her head."

"What the devil got into Old Man Coffee?" Horse demanded.

"Whatever it was got into him, it's going to cost us plenty."

"I don't believe he knows a horse track from a hound's ear," Dunn declared angrily. "He puts me in mind of some old moss-horn—he paws and blows and hollers, but what's he know about it when he gets through? Nothing."

"I'm not so sure," Billy Wheeler said.

"Name one thing he found out!"

"He figured out that the murdered man was not Magoon."

Horse snorted his disgust. "I don't believe it. Coffee thought he had to say something, so he said the first thing come into his head. Every sign we got points to the fact that Lon Magoon was killed, in his own saddle, and on his own horse, and at Short Crick."

"I'm thinking now," said Billy Wheeler, "that we can prove that one way or the other—right here and now."

"How?"

"We've still got his saddle, haven't we?"

"It's under my bunk."

"Let me see it."

Horse Dunn stared at him irritably for a moment, then picked up a lamp with a jerk, and led the way to the

113

clean bare room in which he lived. By the yellow light of the lamp the fine old saddles on their racks against the wall glinted cleanly from silverwork and steel. Dunn sat down on a box and hooked his elbows on the table behind him.

"Horse, how big a man is this Lon Magoon? About my size?"

"Hell, no! Not by eight inches. Little short wiry feller—put you in mind of a grasshopper, or a flea."

Wheeler hauled out Magoon's saddle. There is something mournful and faintly sinister about a saddle in which a man had died, but they were not thinking about that now. Billy Wheeler measured the length of the stirrup leather with his arm—stirrup in armpit, fingers upon the tree.

"I stand five-eleven," Wheeler said. "Yet these stirrups are too long for me to ride. Horse, the man that rode this saddle was over six feet tall."

Horse came across the room in two strides and dropped to one knee beside Billy. "Damn it, *I know* that's Magoon's hull!"

"You mean it *was* Magoon's hull. You can see the short-rig bends worn into the stirrup leathers. But since then the leathers have been let down long, and laced there with rawhide whang."

Horse Dunn measured the stirrup leathers against his own arm. Then he forked the saddle where it lay, jamming his feet into the stirrups. "Tall as me," he breathed, unbelieving. He stared at the saddle incredulously for several moments. "Do you reckon," he said at last, "that infernal old lion hunter would let down those stirrups, just to get us balled up?"

"Look at the wear on the stirrup leather. The saddle has been ridden since the stirrups were let down."

114

Horse Dunn got up slowly and went back to his seat on the box. For a long time he sat staring at the floor. When at last he drew a deep breath and got up, his movements were those of a man preoccupied.

He got out a roll of adhesive tape, pulled off a boot and woolen sock, and began to tape up the outside of his ankle bone, which appeared to be skinned. "I've got to take a hammer to those spurs," he said, his mind on other things. "Seems like they—"

"Horse—Coffee was right! The man that died in this saddle was not Lon Magoon."

Suddenly Dunn stood up, a shaggy towering figure, staring redly at Billy Wheeler. *"Then, in God's name, who's dead?"*

Wheeler regarded him without expression. Within the hour, a shadowy hunch had come over him. He knew that he had no proof for the thing that was in his mind; yet somehow it stood clear and plain. He went to the fireplace, and picked up an old branding iron that had been in use as a fire poker. He squatted on his heels, and with this sooty iron began to make marks on Dunn's clean-swept floor.

"Saying that the 94 is here," he said, marking a cross, "and Short Crick over here; then here lies that broken badlands called the Red Sleep. Seems to me there used to be a trail across the Red Sleep, leading over to Pahranagat."

"Yes, sure. But—"

Horse Dunn waited; Billy Wheeler studied the floor. "Where would a man be coming from, passing over Short Crick toward the 94? Maybe—Pahranagat?"

"Could," Horse admitted dubiously.

"That little railroad spur ends there."

"Sometimes," Horse Dunn made a sudden

contribution, "Lon Magoon has shipped a few stolen beef carcasses out of Pahranagat."

Wheeler nodded. "From Pahranagat the spur runs down the Little Minto to Plumas, then—let me see—"

"Cheat Creek, Monitor, Sikes Crossing," Dunn supplied; "and so to the main stem."

"And so to the main stem," Wheeler repeated. "And maybe an old-timer, a saddle man, working toward the 94 by train, would figure it was better to come by Pahranagat—and there pick up a horse?"

"He wouldn't gain anything. He'd lose time, even."

"But a saddle-minded man?"

They were silent, and the background of the outer night seemed uncommonly still—perhaps because Old Man Coffee's hounds were gone.

"A saddle-minded man," Wheeler repeated, "coming from—say—Flagstaff." He threw the branding iron into the fireplace; it send up a puff of white ash against the black opening. "Horse, where was Bob Flagg last heard from?"

Dunn's voice came out thickly. "Flagstaff," he said.

CHAPTER SIXTEEN

HORSE DUNN SAT RELAXED , STARING MOROSELY AT the floor. In his eyes a dark fire glowed. Wheeler wondered what ugly and shadowy things the old man was seeing. Perhaps, Wheeler thought, he would not wish to see in his life the like of what Horse Dunn was seeing, as he sat looking at the floor. He waited what seemed a long time, but still Horse Dunn did not speak; until the silence became unbearable to the younger man.

"It isn't so far-fetched as it seems," he defended his

theory. "Bob Flagg is long overdue on this range. He was supposed to be bringing with him better than fifty thousand dollars—in some form. Since Link Bender's crowd has been tampering with the mail, it's pretty likely they knew about Bob Flagg being expected—and what he was carrying. If Bob Flagg is dead—and he sure seems to be missing—it's easy to see where more than one in the Inspiration crowd could have had two reasons for killing him—the fifty thousand for itself, and the bust-up of the 94."

Dunn said tonelessly, "He probably wouldn't bring the money in cash."

"They'd take a chance on that."

"If this is so," Dunn said, "this is the end of the 94."

"Not necessarily. If it's true, we'll at least know where Bob Flagg is."

Horse ran a hand across his eyes and shook his head sharply, as if to clear it. "But still we wouldn't know where the money is," he said finally.

"We have a good chance of finding out. Probably he was bringing the money in some sort of paper, such as a cashier's check. In that case it's safe. This thing has gone against us ever since it started. But it can't go against us much more. Once we get the stampede turned the other way, you'll see the whole thing come clear."

Horse Dunn jerked to his feet with an abrupt impatience. "This is all pipe smoke," he said. "For a minute you threw me up in the air with that bunk. But hell! You figure Bob come here a way no man would ever think of coming. He didn't even let me know—but you figure Bender's crowd knew of it, and headed him off. There's better than a hundred million people in this country, and Bob Flagg is one of 'em, so you figure that maybe it was him got killed!"

"Well, we might anyway check up at Pahranagat. There isn't so much travel up the Little Minto but what we could find out if Bob Flagg came that way."

"I'll send Val Douglas over there tomorrow. I sure don't aim to leave any stone unturned. But if a guess is an inch long, you sure jumped a mile."

"Maybe," Wheeler admitted.

"I guess I'm getting old," Horse Dunn said disgustedly, "old and nervous. And I suppose that's what Link Bender's pack is figuring on—that I got no fight left. By God, I'll show 'em fight!"

"How?"

Dunn paced halfway around the room, like a great bear seeking a way out. Wheeler saw his eye slide over the guns on the wall. "Force that crowd and they'll break," he declared. "That's been proved time and time before. Once their key men go down, the others will cut each other's throats trying to take cover. Then pretty soon the story begins to trickle out. If we can bring it to that we can bring it to gun play. By God, this thing began with the guns, and it'll end with the guns—you watch and see!"

Wheeler was unable to see any point to this. "That would have worked once. It won't work now."

Horse Dunn took a turn of the room and the fighting spirit that flared up in his eyes burned low and smoky again. "This country's gone to hell in a handbasket. I've never asked for any more than justice, and I've dealt out nothing less. But where can you get it now? A man's hands are tied. There was more honesty in the old six-gun than in a thousand courts of so-called law. I'd give 'em their cockeyed country. I'd wash my hands of the whole works, and good riddance—if it wasn't for the girl."

It always came back to Marian. The old man didn't dare lose because of what it meant to the girl; he had labored for her too long, in years that for any other man would have been the twilight years of his life. It seemed to Wheeler that certain women were brought into the world for no other purpose than to break up men—using up their lives, giving nothing in return. His own destiny, in his youth, like Horse Dunn's in his old age, was twisted out of recognition by this one girl.

She came before his eyes now, between himself and Horse Dunn, almost as clearly as if she had really been in the room. Without even closing his eyes he could see each varying shade of the delicate coloring of her skin, the half-veiled depths of her eyes, the pliant flex of her slim body as she rode. He had once seen her hair windblown in the sun, and now the memory of it seemed to drift between his eyes and the light like sun-shot smoke. He could almost feel the soft pressure of her fingers, of her lips—for he had kissed her once, a long time ago, before he hardly knew her at all.

Most clearly of all, though, tonight, he could see her silhouette against the lighted window, as she had stood talking to Val Douglas—about what? Nothing probably—just talking, in order to stand there with the young wagon boss.

Wheeler angered, suddenly and uncontrollably—he did not know whether at Douglas or himself. But it was Horse Dunn who was scorched by the powder flash.

Dunn was saying, "Know what I'd like to do? I'd like to cut out for the Argentine. Where a man's cows have a chance to turn around, by God. I'd—"

"Argentine, hell!" Billy exploded at him. "If I'd been running this outfit, this situation would never have come up or started to come up!"

119

"I suppose you'd have sold out," Dunn said, a hard edge on his voice.

"Maybe and maybe not. But I wouldn't have gone cow crazy, range crazy, until I couldn't afford to work my stock!"

"What do you know about how my stock is worked?" Horse roared at him.

"I'll tell you how your stock is worked! No vaccine against Red Water in the lower valley cienegas, where it's wet in spring. A third of the calves unbranded and without guard against black leg. No calves weaned, no heifers kept clear of the main herds, no salt on half the uplands; not a branding chute or a dehorning iron in a hundred miles. Nowadays every calf counts—and you don't even know how many you own!"

"I'll hire no mobs of dudey cowboys to play nurse girl to cows!" Dunn thundered.

Wheeler already knew Dunn's dream of a re-established cow kingdom, vast and open—cattle and horses under one brand over half a dozen counties—half way across the desert state. He could see the grandeur, the raw power of that dream—its homesick reaching back for great things that were gone.

But he saw the other side of it, too. New methods had come to fit new days. Saddle and rope were as important as ever, but beef grades, cow finance, marketing—these were different now.

"Look at the result," Wheeler slammed at him. "Death losses of near thirty per cent last year! Runt bulls in your breeding herds; cows dropping a calf one year out of two or three; the hills full of coyotes, and the Spotted Range full of Texas tick! In another ten years the 94 brand will mark the poorest beef in the west. That's what's the matter here!"

Strangely, Horse did not anger. Wheeler saw that the Old Man thought his tirade was merely based on youth and ignorance, which he had seen in unlimited quantities before.

"Maybe," Dunn said now, "you'd have kept the 94 a little one-horse spread—in the best of shape. But that ain't the question now. We're where we are, and there's no use fighting over what went before."

"I can save it yet," Wheeler told him rashly. "I can throw a hundred thousand into the 94."

"I didn't know you could swing that much. You got it, Billy?"

"What I haven't got of it—I can get."

Horse Dunn studied him, sadly, a long time. "That's an offer, is it?" he said at last.

"On one condition. That you give me a free hand, to hire, fire, buy or sell, land or cattle, for three years."

"I believe," said Dunn, "I'd even do that."

"It's a deal, then?"

"No! You and me'll never make a deal like that!"

"It's your out," Wheeler told him, "and it's your only out. Let me take the finance and the outfit—and all the other ruction falls to pieces."

And now Horse Dunn's eyes blazed again, and his voice crackled. "You'll never put a dime in this brand!"

"It's her brand," Wheeler reminded him. "You willing to let it bust up and go down, and the girl and her mother without a cent?"

"Let 'er bust—before it ever hangs on your dough!"

"But damnation—*why*?"

"You want to know why? I'll tell you why! Because you want that girl! You want that girl—you think I'm blind? But she don't want you. I'd no sooner put her in your debt than I'd sell her to you outright. You're only

121

making the offer because you're in love with Marian."

"You're crazy! I'm making the offer because I think I can come out on it."

"You want the girl," Horse persisted.

"You old fool—" Wheeler held his voice down—"do you think I'd ever expect to get her that way? Do you think I'd want her on the basis of—"

"No, Billy, no. You're not such a fool as that. But you can't help yourself. You couldn't help her feeling that she owed you. Not only for herself. Her mother's mixed up in this."

To Wheeler it seemed that Horse Dunn's viewpoint came out of the worn out conventions and illusions of another day. But there was no use arguing with the old-timer. He tried one more card.

"You've got it wrong, Horse. I don't care any more about her than any other girl out of luck."

Horse Dunn snorted.

"That's all over and done, two years back," Wheeler lied. "Once she could have had me body and soul. But that's all over. I wouldn't tie myself up, not now, to her or anyone else."

"You lie," said Horse calmly.

"Horse, if you'll let me take—"

"Never a dime of your money in her brand," Horse said with utter finality.

Wheeler turned in that night feeling old and grim; and he was wondering why he had fought so hard to build a stake that was useless to him now.

CHAPTER SEVENTEEN

HORSE DUNN'S COW OUTFIT, SHORT-HANDED AS IT was, never wasted much daylight, but Billy Wheeler was anxious to ride out to join Old Man Coffee unquestioned and unaccompanied. Setting a mental alarm clock, he was afoot an hour before the rest of the outfit. It was still dark as he let himself noiselessly into the cook shack and lighted a lamp. He found himself cold biscuits; and in a huge pot on the back of the stove he found bitter coffee above a banked fire.

He had about finished washing down his cold biscuits when he was annoyed to discover that another early riser was about. Someone was walking quietly toward the cook shack. Hurriedly he blew out his light, gulped down half a cup of dregs, and let himself out of the kitchen, anxious to be on his way without conversation.

Then, rounding the corner of the cook shack he almost ran into Marian.

"Morning, Billy." He saw that she was wearing belted overalls and boots.

"Isn't this pretty early? Couldn't you sleep?"

"Not very much. Aren't you going to help me find some breakfast?"

"You bet I am." They went into the cook shack, and he lighted the lamp again. "I'm sorry you had a punk night. But naturally, after that thing that happened, where the—window got shot out—I'm sorry it happened. I'm sorry we couldn't—"

Marian almost whispered, "I'm not sorry."

He stared at her. He would never have guessed, by the lamplight, that she had not slept well. She looked as fresh as dew on wild clover, as clearly fragrant as mustang mint. Only the dark blue of her eyes was misty; and there was something new in her eyes that he did not remember, and did not understand.

"Maybe some day I'll tell you why I'm—glad. I can't tell you now."

Moving slowly, as he quietly shoved wood into the banked fire, got bacon into a skillet, he wondered if she was friendly to that bullet because it had put her in Val Douglas' arms.

"I'm sure sorry I can't stay while this cooks," he said. "But I've got to make a ride."

"Maybe I'll go with you."

"I'm afraid," he said gently, "you wouldn't want to do that."

"You mean you don't want me."

"It isn't that. But—"

"If you had any imagination you'd know I got up at this unearthly hour because I want to talk to you."

He waited, disturbed. She stood close to him, talking almost in whispers. He knew he must get going, but he could not bring himself to move away.

"You see—I heard part of what you and Uncle John said last night."

"You heard—what?"

"Uncle John has a voice like old Rock in full cry," she explained. "My room isn't next to his, but it isn't far away. And when he's angry, I'll bet he can be heard ten miles back into the Tuscaroras. I couldn't help hearing what you said about Bob Flagg being dead. And if that's true—"

Wheeler was startled. "Marian—" he looked at her square—"what else did you hear?"

Her eyes did not waver. "That was all."

124

He thought he detected a faint wicked gleam in her eyes, but he kept his face expressionless, and stood pat.

"We've got to find Old Man Coffee," she said.

"Seems like he's left, Marian."

"We've got to find him. I don't think he's gone so far that it can't be done. I can't imagine his leaving the country until he knows more about this case than he does. The curiosity in that old man is simply terrific."

"That may be," Wheeler admitted. He was worried, dawn could not be far off, and the whole 94 would begin to stir with the first light. He kept listening for sounds of rousing in the bunk house.

"If Bob Flagg is dead," Marian said, "it's a terrible thing for Uncle John."

"It's you will be the loser, Marian, when the 94 goes down."

She made an impatient gesture. "Mother and I will get along all right. Thousands of girls make their own way in this country. Do you think I'd be afraid of it?"

"I don't think I ever saw you afraid of anything."

"But Uncle John is old. We forget that; on a horse, working cattle, he seems like a young man. But he's really old—very old; he's just one of those men who keep going full speed to the end of their lives—and at the end just suddenly break up, all at once. And Billy, the 94 is everything he has in his life."

Billy Wheeler looked into her grave, sweet eyes, and thought of telling her that she might be mistaken; that she herself perhaps meant more to Horse Dunn than a million cattle, or the rise and fall of ten such brands as the 94. For Horse Dunn could not have built his cow kingdom dream into an all-absorbing religion if the whole project had not been given light and color by her own existence. Wheeler was certain that if Marian ever

125

definitely turned her back upon Horse Dunn, the 94 cow kingdom would go to pieces of its own accord.

"It can't be true that Bob Flagg is dead," Marian said almost passionately. "We've got to find out the truth and prove the truth."

"Not so easily done, Marian."

"Old Man Coffee can do it. I know he's only human, and he's superstitious about his dogs. But he can find out who's been killed—I'm certain he can."

"If Horse hadn't quarreled with him—"

"It's too late to patch that up. But if only I can talk to Old Man Coffee I'm sure I can persuade him to do this one thing. But, Billy, you'll have to help me."

"I don't know what I can do, Marian. Coffee doesn't take any special stock in me."

"You've got to take me to him," the girl said. "You can find him—I know you can find him."

"What makes you think so?"

"Can't you?"

Wheeler hesitated; what Old Man Coffee had told him had been in confidence. Yet, invariably, he found it almost impossible to speak untruly to this girl.

His hesitation was fatal. "You know where he is," she said suddenly.

He picked up his bridle. "I've got to get out of here."

"Billy—you're riding out to meet Old Man Coffee!"

"Tell your uncle I'll be back tonight," he said abruptly, and moved toward the door.

"I'm going with you."

"I'm sorry," he said, "but you're not. You're a pest, that's what you are! Go on and eat your breakfast."

Yet he knew that he could not bluff this girl, nor control anything that she did; and what was worse, she knew it too. As he left her she was writing a note to her

126

uncle, telling him where she had gone; and she was with him, mounted on her own pony, as he left the layout.

"I suppose he told you not to bring anyone with you," she said when they had jogged a silent mile. "Well, I don't count."

"If you beat your own purpose by your cussed stubbornness." he said morosely, "don't blame me."

"I'll answer for it."

They rode an hour in silence, and a second hour, while the sun came up and drenched the gaunt hills with unbelievable color—crimson, rose, and dusky blues edged with clean gold. There was a clean cool smell in the air, as if the pounding heat of the summer would soon be gone; and nothing in the bright quiet of that country suggested the smash of guns and the acrid sting of powder smoke, or the dark angry struggles that this range had seen, would see again.

Wheeler pressed his pony along steadily, eyes to the front; and he was combatting his keen awareness that the girl was at his side. He had loved this gaunt, clear-colored country of blasting sun and sharp shadows; differently than he had loved the girl, but as a man loves his home. But now he knew he would need another different country, a new type of grazing land, if he was ever going to forget this girl who rode beside him, whom he could never possess. There would always be a mocking loneliness in these desert spaces, something sad and mad in the empty shimmering dance of the heat devils on these red rocks; and he promised himself that when the 94 difficulties were settled—one way or the other—this land would never have a chance to torment him again. He thought of Horse Dunn's mention of the Argentine, and wondered if the Argentine cattle grazed vast desert ranges, such as this.

They were almost in the shadow of Lost Whiskey Butte when she broke the silence between them.

"Billy—I told you something that wasn't so."

He waited.

"It was when we were talking about Bob Flagg, and how I heard what you and Uncle John said about that. And I said that was all I heard. Well—that wasn't all."

"What else did you hear?"

"I heard—it all."

Unexpectedly he found it difficult to tell himself that it didn't matter. He was able to hear again his own words of last night to Horse Dunn; "Once she could have had me body and soul; but that's all over. I couldn't tie myself up, not now, to her or anybody else." He wondered why he was so sorry that he had ever spoken that lie at all. Things being as they were, it couldn't make any difference. But now he realized that she was waiting for him to answer, and he managed to say, "That's all right."

"Isn't it better," she said, "that we both know now how things really stand—between us, I mean?"

He made himself say, "I guess so, Marian."

"It *is* better," she said, and he wondered why her voice seemed so sad. "Because—don't you see?—there's nothing to keep us from being friends now—really friends. And each of us—all of us—are going to need what friendliness there is left in the world, I think."

"No doubt of that," he said, just because it seemed he was supposed to say something.

"For some reason—I can't tell you why—I have the strangest feeling about this day; as if there's something terrible ahead of us, so terrible that nothing is ever going to be just the same again."

This time he didn't answer. In the sharp light of the

morning his own reasoning seemed clearer and stronger than it had seemed the night before; and he thought he knew what was ahead.

She swung her horse nearer his, and though no more than the leather of her tapadero touched his stirrup bow, he put his hands together on the reins, to steady them.

"Can't we be friends, truly, as if—two years ago had never happened?"

He tried to relax the grim set of his face, but something behind his face was dark, and bitter. He was afraid to meet her eyes, and kept his own on the loom of Lost Whiskey Butte, ahead. "Why, of course, Marian."

"You promise me?"

"Sure."

She held out her hand and he took it as he would have taken the hand of a man. For a moment her fingers pressed and clung. Vaguely, he knew that she had need of him, in her own way.

CHAPTER EIGHTEEN

As Coffee with his dogs about him, rode out to meet Wheeler and Marian Dunn from Lost Whiskey Butte, the girl pushed her horse ahead. She stopped close to the old man, facing him squarely.

"He tried to keep me from coming," she told Coffee, "but there wasn't anything he could really do. Now, if you want me to go back, I will."

Old Man Coffee grinned. Wheeler had wondered how Old Man Coffee would take Marian's unexpected appearance at the rendezvous. But now it seemed to Billy that he himself was the outsider. "What's this lout doing here?" Coffee asked, jerking his head at Billy.

"He isn't a lout."

Coffee moved his mule nearer Marian's pony, and leaned forward to peer into her eyes. Then he laid a bony old hand on her shoulder. "Child, what happened to you?"

"Nothing."

"Something did, though," Wheeler contradicted. He told Coffee of the shot from the brush.

The old hunter scowled; he looked as nearly startled as they had even seen him look. "This changes the whole set-up," he complained. "I thought I had it licked. But—this smears it."

"I don't follow that," Marian said.

"Neither do I," Coffee said, dismissing discussion. He turned to Wheeler. "You told her what we aimed to try?"

"No."

"Well, you should have. This is a kind of a sad, dark job we're on today, girl. We're going to try to find the—the man that was killed at Short Crick."

"I guessed that," Marian said.

"But you come anyway. Huh! Seems like there's more to you than meets the eye. But don't you think you better go back? For one thing, there's going to be an awful lot of riding to this job, child."

"I'll stick till I'm sent back."

"Well, I wouldn't downright send you back—yet."

Old Man Coffee led off to the northeast, his sleepy-eared mule in an ambling shuffle, and they rode in silence for a little way. Coffee signaled to them to come abreast.

"Maybe you've wondered some," he said, "why I've been kind of prowling around of nights, as your wagon boss was at pains to make known. Well, I guess it won't

130

hurt nothing to tell how a thing like this is done. Did you ever listen to coyote voices, of a night, Marian?"

"I couldn't very well help it, could I?"

"There's a funny thing about them. More things interest coyotes than you'd expect. And if something kind of strange and interesting happens on the range, all of 'em know it, all over the desert. We'd learn queer things from 'em if we could understand their talk a little better."

Old Man Coffee let his keen, deep-set old eyes drift along the horizon land marks. "One of the things a coyote takes interest in," he said, "is a man that's dead."

The brassy desert-sun was high by then, pouring an incredible eye-stunning light upon all that vast range; but even there in all that brilliance of daylight a queer cold chill touched the back of Marian's neck as she listened to the gaunt old lion hunter.

"Not that it's any of their business," Coffee went on. Coyotes won't touch a dead man; neither will a loafer wolf. But they'll circle around, and kind of wail, and sing. Once before this I found out where a corpse was hid by listening to the coyotes voices at night."

"I've heard of that," said Billy Wheeler; "but I took it to be the bunk."

"It's pretty hard with coyotes," said Coffee, "because there's so many of 'em, and they talk so much. Mighty hard, too, to tell what way the yapping comes from. This time, though, we got a break. There's a loafer wolf on the range. He'll only talk about certain things, and maybe speak only two, three times in a week. So when he lets out the same kind of queer cry, in the same place three or four nights in a row, a man begins to wonder."

Coffee's matter of fact words conjured up a strange piclure of the old lion hunter standing alone out on the

131

night desert, listening to weird ghostly voices far off—
the voices of animals that drifted like shadows through
some lost rift of brush, and talked about a man who was
dead.

"That," said Marian, "is the most fantastic thing I
ever heard!"

"Not so crazy when you think how much goes on that
them critters know, but we never hear of. Funny thing is
that it's so few times a man learns something by them—
unless it's something about the weather, or some such
simple thing."

That was a long day, and a strange day—the strangest
in Marian Dunn's life. Their work carried them a great
distance, much of which was wasted in quartering, and
the long following of false trails. Some queer geometry
of land marks was working in Coffee's head, but what it
was like they could not guess, and he did not explain.
Repeatedly Old Man Coffee pulled the dogs off
invisible trails which he declared were those of coyotes.
It was after noon before a new note came into the
howling of the hounds, signaling the trail of the loafer
wolf.

"This loafer trail," said Old Man Coffee, "is three
days old. I don't reckon it'll serve."

It did not serve, though Coffee let it lead them seven
miles in no particular direction before he pulled off the
dogs. After that they picked up other trails, presumably
of the same loafer, though perhaps of another, trails that
were lost again, or discarded. Twice Old Man Coffee
urged the girl to turn back, but she would not. Marian's
face was white with the fatigue a jog-trotting horse can
impose on unaccustomed muscles by the time the day
drew to a close.

The sun had gone down behind the Tuscaroras, and

the long grey dusk was on the range as they came on to the broken wilderness of upthrust red rock that was known as the Red Sleep. The dogs were voicing uncertainty here, obviously running no trail, though Old Man Coffee seemed to know where he was going. And now old Rock made a curious play. The old dog had been in a sulk all day long, unwilling to quarter the trail of the loafer wolf; but now he sent up a long full-throated cry and drifted swiftly, nose down, a hundred yards along the red rock.

Old Man Coffee said under his breath, "I'll be eternally damned!" Abruptly the old dog turned to look at Old Man Coffee, let his tail drop again, and quit the trail.

"What's the matter?"

"Everything," Coffee said. "I never done so much false figuring in my life!" He pushed ahead quickly now, shouting to his hounds, jerking new life into them with gutteral Indian words that the others did not understand.

Now suddenly the big spotted hound that had usurped old Rock's place as leader sprang ahead, bawling; and in another moment the rest of the hounds were with him, running full cry, out-distancing the horses.

"The wolf again," said Coffee, a new keen edge on his voice. "Children, we're near the end of the trail!"

Yet because the trail of the wolf was indirect and circling, they spent another hour in following the dogs. The ponies were scrambling over broken rock now, keeping up as best they could. The dusk was very deep when Old Man Coffee pulled up at last and sat waiting.

They did not see what had stopped him at first; but after a few moments they saw that the hounds had made a circle and were coming back. Coffee got down off his mule, called in his dogs, and tied up each of them, separately, to rock or scrub oak. But he had to crack the long dog whip over them more than once before they would lie down, sulking and moaning in their throats. Old Rock, the only one untied, lay down under the feet of the mule, raised his nose to heaven, and let out a long deep-chested wail.

Old Man Coffee tightened his saddle. "Marian," he said, "this is as far as you go."

The girl's face was white in the dusk and her eyes were wide and dark. Until Wheeler saw that, he had not realized that here in the high heart of the Red Sleep they found themselves in a gaunt and terrible country. The sky was still pallid, but the Red Sleep was in utter shadow; and the vast uprearing chunks of rock, unearthly in their sheer mass, seemed to loom over them murderously, bearing their spirits down. He knew that Marian could never before have seen anything like the dark, terrible desolation of this place. For a moment, as he looked at Marian, he thought that she faintly swayed.

"Wouldn't you like to get down and rest?"

"I'd rather sit here."

Old Man Coffee studied her for a moment. "You stay with her Billy. I don't know how long this will take."

He said something unintelligible to the dogs, and moved away from them, the dainty feet of his mule picking its way, and old Rock slinking close behind. Within the hundred yards he had disappeared. For a little while the "clop" of his mule's feet came to them, echoing queerly so that it seemed to come sometimes from one side, sometimes from another. Then this died away, and except for the occasional eerie moaning of a hound, the silence of death was on the Red Sleep.

They sat there for what seemed like an endless time.

Billy Wheeler tried to talk to break that sad terrible stillness, but this place smothered the words in his throat. When he managed to speak his voice sounded hushed and strange, and the girl made no reply. They sat and waited a long, an interminable time.

The first stars were showing when Old Man Coffee came back to them at last, his black mule moving like a lean tall shadow among shadows. He came close to them, then for a moment sat silent, looking back over his shoulder the way he had come; and Wheeler knew that he was futilely seeking words for what he had to say.

Long before the old man spoke they knew he had found what he had sought.

"It's Bob Flagg," Old Man Coffee said.

CHAPTER NINETEEN

HORSE DUNN ACCEPTED THE NEWS THAT FLAGG WAS dead more quietly, more steadily, than Wheeler had expected. He had pictured Horse Dunn raising clenched hands to heaven and shouting anathema. Instead Dunn stood grim and silent; his eyes were lost somewhere in the dark distance, and deep within them a smoky fire burned. But when he spoke it was quietly.

"How was he killed?" Dunn asked at last.

"By a shotgun; the same as Cayuse Cayetano."

"Where's Coffee?"

Coffee, Wheeler had found, could not be persuaded to return with them to the 94. It was Coffee's belief that Dunn had made a serious mistake when he had chosen to hold Magoon's saddle instead of turning it in to the sheriff. Coffee did not propose to be mixed up in a similar mistake regarding the long-sought *corpus delicti*. He therefore turned the head of his mule toward Inspiration, determined to report his discovery to Sheriff Walt Amos at once.

When Wheeler had explained this to Horse, the cow boss was silent again. Undoubtedly the old fighter was searching in his mind for some way in which guns and battle could be brought to bear against the forces which were closing in upon him and upon the brand he had built. But as yet there was no play for the only type of weapon the old fighter truly understood. He stood like a trapped silvertip, praying only for one more chance to smash out at his enemies. But what other things the old man was seeing as he stared off into the night, Wheeler could not know.

"The sheriff will be out here in the morning, sure," Wheeler said. "I think Walt Amos means to be fair. But there's better than a hundred men in Inspiration, all out of outfits that hate the 94. Amos is sitting on a stove, and it's getting hotter every minute."

"Let him come."

"Any more dope on the Cayetano killing?"

"I sent Gil Baker to Ace Springs. But he hasn't come back."

"Val Douglas went to Pahranagat, did he?"

"He left this morning. I suppose it'll be late tomorrow night before he gets back—maybe longer. Steve and Tulare and me, we spent the day prospecting around in the Tuscarora foothills, here."

"And didn't find anything," Wheeler supposed.

"Billy," said Horse Dunn, "there's somebody been slinking around over there. We found the ashes of two different fires. And I'm not a damn bit sure there isn't somebody prowling around there yet."

136

"Now who the devil would that be?"

"That's just it—we don't know who that would be. I guess—it doesn't matter, now."

"I'm trying to think," Billy Wheeler said, "why somebody would be hanging around in the Tuscarora foothills, keeping himself under cover; and I can't think of any reason."

"There's bloody hands in Link Bender's crowd," Dunn said, his voice flat and heavy with bitterness. "Just as sure as powder and lead spell death."

"Well, but why should one of them fire into the layout, like that bushwacker did last night? They've got us going and coming, any way; what's the idea of getting in a hurry?"

"That I can't answer," said Dunn. "God in heaven! If I could only have ten days to work this thing out, I bet I'd lay hands on that killer!"

But they did not have ten days—or even one. It was hard for Billy Wheeler to believe that he had been at the 94 only four days—that Bob Flagg had been dead less than a week. The thing had swept over them like a rock slide, all at once. The bitter enmity against Horse Dunn and his brand had done that. It was an enmity that had bided its time for years, and now flamed up sharply, forcing the rush of events, on the first hint of opportunity to crush Horse Dunn.

They had expected Sheriff Walt Amos to appear in the course of the night, or at least no later than the first light; but it was noon before Amos appeared.

Amos, though definitely not a coward, was a cautious man. Though he had chosen deputies who were bitter enemies of Horse Dunn, he recognized and feared the spark-and-powder possibilities wherever these men were brought face to face with the turbulent old warrior

137

of the 94. So Walt Amos again came alone, as he had come after Billy Wheeler.

At the 94 he found only Horse Dunn and Billy Wheeler, for Steve Hurley and Tulare Callahan were in the Tuscaroras in search of the unknown prowler now believed to be hiding there; Val Douglas and Gil Baker had not yet returned; and Marian was out with her pony. Walt Amos climbed out of his car and walked slowly to the gallery of the cook shack, where the 94 people happened to be. They awaited him in silence.

"Horse," said Walt Amos, "the time has come when I can't put off acting no more."

"What have you done with Gil Baker?" Horse Dunn demanded.

"He's in Inspiration. We had to take him in."

"Is he hurt?"

"Not bad. He came prowling around Ace Springs, where Cayetano was killed, and one of the deputies hollered to him to halt, but he made a run for it. They had to throw down on him before he'd give himself up. Turned out he was shot in the leg."

"You're getting almighty high-handed around here, Amos!"

"Sorry. But I reckon it's going to seem still a little more so. Dunn, I got to take you in."

"On what charge?"

"Held for questioning; concerning murder."

Horse Dunn stood up, his thumbs hooked in his belt, and his eyes rolled slowly over the foothills of the Tuscaroras; it seemed to Wheeler that he was looking for a sign.

"I know what you're thinking, Dunn," Walt Amos said. "Feeling is sure running pretty high in Inspiration. But there's going to be no necktie parties out of my jail.

138

When I let you walk out of Inspiration, day before yesterday, it wasn't because I didn't think I could hold the jail; it was because I didn't want to have to shoot into any mob of cowmen. But I think they understand about that now. I promise you this: if ever it comes to a pinch, I'll give you your guns."

Now Dunn answered him at last, and Wheeler saw that somehow, in the course of the night, the old man had been able to prepare himself for this thing. His voice came thickly, as if the words were almost too much for him, but the belligerence of the man was buried very deep. "When you want to move out?" he asked.

"I'd like to get on back as soon as you're ready, Dunn. Only, first I'll have to ask your leave to take a look around this place. I've got a search warrant for that, if you want to see it."

Dunn studied him curiously. "You come here all alone," he said queerly, "and you just casually ask my leave to search my place. Amos, I never expected to see the like of that."

"I ain't hardly figuring you aim to stop me, Dunn."

"Go ahead and search your head off."

"Give me your keys, and you folks stay here."

"There ain't any keys to anything around here."

The sheriff crossed the dusty space between the cook shack and the ranch house, and disappeared in the house. And they waited. Horse Dunn sat on the edge of the gallery floor, his back against a post, his hands locked around one knee. He sat impassive, except for that persistent smoulder deep in his eyes; but neither Marian nor Billy Wheeler would have wanted to speak to him then.

And now out of a trail that wound through the tall

139

buckbrush back of the layout a rider came. His horse was at a quiet running walk, but the animal shone wet with sweat, and from under the edges of the saddle blanket the lather rolled. It was Tulare Callahan.

He rode directly to the cook shack gallery and swung down. "Where's the sheriff?" he asked in an undertone.

"He's ransacking the dump," Dunn said in a flat voice.

"I seen him come in," said Tulare, "and I lay out to see what was the play. Horse, I've seen Lon Magoon!"

"Tulare, are you sure?"

"We only sighted him far off on a high ridge, at better'n a mile. But Horse, I knew him as sure as I know my name. His horse looked like that good sorrel of ours, we call Brandy. We signed him to come and talk, but he sloped. We took out after him hell for leather—Steve Hurley's trying to trail him yet—but he got loose about four miles up the Tamale Vine. I knew you was looking for the Sheriff; and I thought you might want to know this, if you was still here."

"Thanks, Tulare. Tell you what you do. Take—"

They were interrupted by the approach of the sheriff, who came toward them now from the house. He looked as if he had found what he was after. "There's just a couple things I got to take back with us, Dunn," he said apologetically. "I got to take them three shotguns of yours, and your shell loading outfit, with all the powder and shot. And naturally I got to take Magoon's saddle."

"Make free with anything you please," Dunn said without expression.

"You taking us all in, Amos?" Tulare asked.

"I guess just one will be plenty, this trip, Callahan."

"Amos," said Horse Dunn, "I'm going to have to ask for a little more time."

140

The sheriff looked doubtful. "Well, I don't suppose an hour or two—"

"Thirty hours," Dunn said.

Amos sbook his head. "No—I can't do that."

"Amos," said Dunn, "from the first, you've played into the hands of the people that are against the 94. That's your lookout, if you want to do that; I don't figure to make any trouble for you in any way. But I got to have today and tomorrow to put my affairs straight. You give me thirty hours and I give you my word I'll go with you tomorrow night."

"I don't question your word, Dunn," Amos said. "But I doubt if the people of the county will stand for it. They're sure hollering for an arrest."

"It's you that's sheriff," Dunn pointed out. "This is the last thing I'm going to ask of you. But I sure got to have until tomorrow night."

Sheriff Amos studied him, and appeared to consider for a long time. "I want to be fair, Dunn," he said. "Public opinion is awful strong against you—stronger than is reasonable, in a way. This isn't an easy thing for me to do. You know that."

"Tomorrow night," Dunn said stubbornly.

"Tomorrow night, then," the sheriff agreed at last.

CHAPTER TWENTY

HORSE DUNN WATCHED THE DUST OF THE SHERIFF'S car settle reluctantly upon the dry flats until he was sure Walt Amos was on his way.

"Saddle up," he ordered. "Get a fresh horse, Tulare."

Out at the corrals they roped square-built, hill-running ponies. "Horse," Billy said, "how big a fool is

141

Magoon?"

"Magoon's a queer one, all right. If it weren't for that I'd say he must be clear of the killings, or why ain't he in Mexico by now? But he hasn't got all of his buckles—and that's a break for us. Because we sure need to catch us a witness."

Tulare put in, his mouth full of bread and meat he had grabbed from the kitchen, "Witness, hell! I bet he shotgunned Flagg himself, for the dough he had on him. He probably sold Flagg the horse and saddle in Pahranagat, then rode along with him, waiting his chance. Then later he downed Cayuse because Cayuse caught up to him. Get it?"

"I can't swaller any set-up that doesn't show the Link Bender crowd at the bottom of it," Horse Dunn said flatly.

"Even that fits in," Tulare insisted. "I bet it was them tipped off Magoon on the dough Flagg was toting."

"Then who threw that rifle shot in here night before last?" Wheeler objected.

"Maybe Magoon did it. Ain't I said he was crazy?"

"You figure he's packing a rifle and a shotgun, both?"

"Might be carrying four or five guns and a kitchen stove too. When a guy's nuts, all rules is off."

"Coffee figured there was a third man at Short Crick."

"I think Coffee's full of Injun brew."

Dunn grunted. "Best bet we've got is grab this cow thief and see if he yells. We'll try, anyway." He jerked tight his latigo. "Magoon is most likely headed out of the country. But here's what we do: Tulare, you got the fastest horse. You circle to the head of the Tamale Vine, by way of the upper bench, and try to beat Magoon to the Pass. If you see Steve send him southwest through that runt timber. If Magoon goes out that way he'll water his horse at that little lake on the other side."

"Most likely Steve was drawed over into Mormon Crater."

"Then I'll find him, because that's where I'm going. Billy, you strike northwest into the point country. There's a bare chance that Magoon will skirt along the foothills, picking a pass north of where we're figuring on. Get yourself a good high lookout, and camp there until tomorrow."

"This is as good a try as any," Tulare approved.

"Then let 'er buck! And if either of you meet up with Marian, you send her home a-packing. Billy, leave word with Tia Cara where we've gone." He put his horse out of the layout at a sharp jog, Tulare beside him.

Wheeler held back long enough to urge his horse to drink, and get himself a canteen; then he also struck out, northward, along the outer edge of the brush. Two hours before dusk he took his post on a high rocky point far to northward of the 94. He hid his horse, sprawled with his back against a hot rock, and swept the rolling country. Quickly his eye picked out the trails a rider would follow in moving from the Tamale Vine toward the northwest passes. Far out on the dusty flats he could make out dots that were cattle; but in all that vast visible range he could find no mounted man, and nothing moved on the trails he watched.

Dusk came on, cool and clear and utterly still, and after a long time the twilight faded, slowly giving way to the faint light of appearing stars, and Wheeler had sighted no one. An hour before dawn he was watching again, waiting the first light. But morning showed only the same vast empty range; and three hours after sun-up

143

he knew he must give it up.

He saddled his pony and dropped down from his lookout. One by one he sought out and examined the trails he had picked as the ones Magoon might use. This took time; trails easily visible from his high lookout were many slow miles apart for a rider on the ground. Still he found no sign; and he at last turned toward the 94, disgusted. It was deep into the afternoon by the time his thirst-fretted pony brought him in.

Marian came running out to him as he unsaddled.

"In heaven's name," said Wheeler, "where were you yesterday?"

"I was out with my horse—what of it? When's Uncle John coming back?"

"He'll be back by tonight; he gave Amos his word. Steve and Tulare sighted Lon Magoon up—"

"Tia Cara told me all that. But look here—where in the world are they hunting for him now? I've ridden all over these hills back here and never saw a sign of them."

"They're probably hunting a little farther than you went."

"Then," she said, "they're hunting too far away! Because I'm sure I saw Lon Magoon—not more than three hours ago."

Much riding and the heat of the day had made Wheeler drowsy, but now he snapped sharply awake. "What did he look like?"

"A scraggly little man with a rifle in his hands; he was on a good sorrel with a blaze face and one white leg."

"Good lord! Did he see you?"

"I don't think so. After he was out of sight I got back here as fast as I could. I was praying somebody would be here. But I've been here over an hour. I thought nobody was ever going to come."

"I guess—can you find the place where he was?"

"Of course."

It cost fresh ponies an hour's hard work to take them to the place where Marian had seen the armed rider; yet Wheeler was astonished. The 94 riders were casting wide, blocking off distant passes—and if Marian was right, Magoon had doubled back to take cover almost under their own roof. Marian led Billy to a vast, V-cut gulch, in a country heavy with desert juniper and scrub oak.

"He was riding down here, headed west. I was in those upper ledges."

In the broad canyon the ground was flinty, but in the bottom a slender ribbon of gravelly sand wound a crooked course, marking the run-off of last winter's rains. Working up-canyon, Wheeler presently found what he was after: the trail of a horse crossing a twist in the sands of the vanished creek.

"Marian—you sure seem to have done what failed us all! Can you read that trail?"

"No."

"A tired horse, unshod, ridden over rocks for three, four days; trying to hurry, plugging along steadily, and straight—"

He let his voice trail off. Some isolated memory from far back was troubling him, trying to make itself known. He knew this place; once before, years ago, he had ridden here, but only once, for the poor feed called few cattle. He remembered bitter, soapy-tasting water.

Suddenly he remembered. "There's some sort of old shelter up here—some fool mining men had it once. There's a little water there, not much good, and stock

145

can't get at it; riders don't go through there once a year. Marian, if I can work this right—we've got him!"

"He has nearly three hours' start, Billy."

"But his horse is close to played out. He'll figure to hide out up there and rest. If I can come on him before dark I can catch him in a straight run."

Marian's eyes shone with a queer, fearful light. "Now? Tonight?"

"Right now—within the four miles."

"You *will* be careful,—won't you?"

"Sure. By the time you get back to the ranch your uncle should be there. Tell him—"

"By the time *I* get back?"

"Of course—he told Amos he'd be back. Tell him to send somebody with a fresh led horse. I'm going to—"

"But I'm not going back."

He stared at her a moment. "You sure are going back! What are you talking about?"

"I found this trail," she said with an odd, tremulous stubbornness, "and I mean to follow it out."

"Look here, Marian! This man is mixed up somehow with the killing of Bob Flagg. He may even be guilty himself. For all we know, he'll fight like a cornered wolf."

"I'm going on," she said again.

Wheeler saw that the girl was grave, nervous. He said suddenly, "Are you afraid to ride back alone?"

"If you were going back, I would still go up this trail."

"In God's name, Marian, what's the matter with you?"

"Nothing's the matter with me."

She was pale and quiet, and she sat very still in her saddle; but, strangely, he thought he had never seen her

146

more alive. Suddenly it seemed to him that a great unsuspected strength linked this girl to the desert hills; and that behind it perhaps lay fires he had never seen.

But the twilight was deepening in the broad reaches of the canyon, and little time was left. Even a worn-out horse could get away if the dark closed down. "Take my word for it," he said brusquely, "you're going back—now, right now!"

"Are you ordering me?"

"Call it that."

"I think," she said, "you can't do that."

"You think I can't?"

"What can you do?"

For a moment it seemed to him that there was nothing he could do. In the face of an immediate necessity he found himself helpless. Then it occurred to him that there might, after all, be one way, only one. His mouth and eyes set hard, and he kicked his pony sideways, close to hers.

"You think I can't send you out of this?" he said.

He leaned out of his saddle and with one arm clamped her hard against him. With the other hand he turned her face upward; and he kissed her mouth, certain that she would ride with him no farther.

For a moment she was motionless except that he felt a sharp quiver run through her body, and her lips trembled under his. Since the first—only—time he had kissed her, two years ago, he had thought that he could never forget the soft warmth of her lips, the fragile resilience of her slim body; but now the actuality of the girl in his arms half stunned him, she had been untouchable as a dream for so long. He thought he swayed in the saddle, and the twilight about them turned suddenly dark and unreal. A strand of her fine hair touched his eyes, lightly as the touch of a breath; he felt the faint pulsation of her breast. He did not know that his arm tightened about her so that he almost broke her in two.

Then her body twisted and she struck spurs to her pony, so that he had to release her to avoid dragging her out of the saddle. His voice shook with the curbed pressure of an emotion he mistook for anger as he said savagely, "Now go on back!"

She sat a little apart from him, and her pony stood head high, very shaky from the sharp unsteadiness of her hand upon the curb. She said, "I suppose that's the bitterest thing that ever happened to me. Can't you ever do anything but hurt and destroy and break up?"

"Will you go back?" he said between his teeth.

"No! I most certainly will not!"

Her voice was repressed, but there was smoky fire in her eyes, and the upward twitch of her eyebrows as she spoke out of her anger was strangely suggestive of Horse Dunn. He looked her in the eyes, and he knew that he could in no way bend her will. A great sense of fatalism overcame him. This had been his position here ever since the beginning—boxed in without weapons and without choice. Now, unable to manage this girl, he still had to go on. Without a word he turned his pony's head up the gulch.

He put his horse into the soundless sand of the dry stream, and pressed into a shuffling jog; and they rode for a long time, while the slow twilight deepened. Wheeler thought that he had never seen any desert country so bleak and lifeless—not excepting the Red Sleep, where Coffee had found Bob Flagg wrapped in eternal stillness under the red rock. And although Marian's pony trailed close behind his own, it seemed to him that he had never been so utterly alone, in a vacant

148

world. Once as he swung crosswise in his saddle to turn to Marian, he caught her brushing tears from her cheeks with her gloved fingers.

He said in a low voice, "If a gun cracks, go to the ground, and take any cover there is."

They plugged along another mile, while the canyon narrowed. The light was failing fast.

Marian whispered, "Billy!"

He stopped his horse and she came up, stirrup to stirrup. Her eyes were fixed on the high south rim of the gulch. She said almost inaudibly, "There's a rider up there. I saw him cross between those rabbit-ear rocks."

They sat still for a long minute, listening. The gash in the rocks that Marian indicated was no more than a hundred yards away on a high-angled line, and the dusk was very still, but Wheeler could detect no least sound of a walking horse.

"It must have been a trick of the light," Wheeler said.

"Billy, I saw him as plainly as I see you here, now."

He hesitated a moment more, then stepped to the ground.

"Hold my pony."

CHAPTER TWENTY-ONE

BILLY WHEELER'S EYES WERE SWEEPING THE UPPER levels as he stepped out of the saddle. In the ragged brush and upthrust ledges above that forgotten nameless canyon, a thousand horsemen could have been hidden within the quarter mile. His eyes were grim as he passed his reigns to the girl.

"Marian, for the last time—won't anything I can say or do make you go back?"

"No!" She smiled, faintly, a little grim stubborn smile. "You can't seem to understand that I—"

A sharp report sounded above, and Marian's pony suddenly folded at the knees. Its head dropped as if it had been felled with a sledge, its nose stubbed in the sand; it went down on its side like a great sand bag, and was still before the echoes had died from the rifle in the upper rocks. Wheeler's pony reared, tearing free its had, and bolted down the canyon.

He sprang toward Marian. She had swung herself clear, and was already getting up beside her down horse. "Get down—quick, behind the horse!" She hesitated, but he did not. He seized her shoulders, deftly kicked her heels from under her and laid her flat behind her dead pony. "Stay there!"

He pulled his gun and moved five yards to one side, standing up to draw what further fire there might be. A minute passed, two minutes, while he watched for movement on the upper rim; but there was no sound or shot. The desert hills were as silent and empty as before, except for the dying rattle of hoofs down-canyon from Wheeler's stampeding pony.

Marian's voice came to him. "What in the world happened ?"

"Somebody took your pony through the head with a rifle, is all." A crazy red anger was on him. Loose in these hills was a man as dangerous and unaccountable as a wild animal with hydrophobia. For the first time he inclined to Tulare's belief that Magoon was the killer. Too much long riding alone—especially when it was mixed up with the night riders' long rope—could do queer things to a man whose head wasn't too strong in the first place. Lon Magoon, half outlaw, half sneak-thief, all coyote, might have turned at last into something which must be destroyed at sight, without hesitation. He walked to the dead horse and roughly verified the angle of the shot; then turned and began to climb the canyon slope.

"Billy, come back! You can't—"

"You stay down," he ordered her savagely. "Or by God, I'll tie you down with my pigging-string!"

It would have been easy then to walk into gun-fire, easy to shoot it out with an ambushed man. Always keeping his eye on Marian's position, he searched those upper slopes, backward, forward, and quartering. But what happened to him was the one hardest thing of all— to find the broken country empty and silent, with nothing in it to fight or trail. It seemed impossible that any horse could have been ridden here without leaving some small sign, nor that he could not have heard retreating hoofs upon the rocky ledges. But though he walked between the rabbit-ear rocks, where Marian believed she had seen the skulking rider, the hard-baked ground showed no mark of hoof or heel, and there was no sound of movement anywhere.

In the end he could only go back to the girl with no result to show, and no assurance as to what was ahead. He would not have been surprised, when he turned his back on that emptiness, if a gun had spoken from a place where no one was, and brought him down.

"No catchum," he told Marian. She had not stayed under cover, but was sitting on a rock, a little apart from her dead horse. No use quarreling with her over that; she had already proved to him that he couldn't control anything she chose to do. He put himself between her and the rim. "It's a long walk back," he said morosely. "That's my fault. I'm not used to this stuff, or I wouldn't have lost my pony. When I saw your horse

151

drop—I lost my head, I guess."

"Because it was I," she said with an unexpected, deep-striking clarity.

"We'd better get going, I think."

"We can't go on? And get—"

"That must have been the man we were after, that killed your horse."

She drew a deep breath, and stood up. For a moment she looked all about her, upward at the high, towering rims. Then suddenly he saw her sway.

He stepped forward in time to steady her with his hands on her arms. And now he found that she was trembling violently. Her face was white, making her eyes look enormous, and very dark. "Billy—I'm afraid—" She sat down on the rock again, as if her knees would not hold her up.

"No more danger, child. It's all over, and he's gone."

"But who could it be? Why should he want to—hurt me?"

"I—I don't know that. I can't imagine any living thing wanting to hurt you. I swear, by *la Madre de Dios!*—he'll pay for it if I live to find him. Now don't you be afraid any more. It's all over, for now."

The tears began to roll down her face, and she hid them with her hands. Quickly he looked about him, checking the throw of the land. Then he lifted her up and led her to a pocket gully at the foot of the precipitous north slope. When he had made sure that searching lead could not reach them here, he got the blanket from her dead pony, and spread it for her to rest upon; and gathered bits of dead brush to build a tiny fire. "Striking fire kind of seems like setting up a mark," he apologized. "But you're plenty safe if you stay close under the rock split. Now you take it easy. We'll rest here an hour or so; then we'll go back."

Marian drew up her knees, and hid her eyes against them. One of her hands reached out to him uncertainly, and he took it. Her fingers were moist and cold, with a tremor in them; he warmed them between his hands, noticing how huge his hands were made to look by her slim fingers.

Presently she looked up, shook her head sharply, and drew away her hand. "I'm all right now. Did you ever see such silliness?"

"Rest easy. We've got lots of time."

The dusk had closed more rapidly at the last, and little light was left in the sky; but a moon was rising behind a high point of rocks, silhouetting a crag that looked like a horse's head. He noticed how huge it looked, as moons do when they are low to the earth. The horse-head crag had a four-hundred-foot profile, but it looked little against the moon, which was made to look bigger than a mountain, bigger than a range.

"You know," he said, "it's funny how badly things work out; never the way you want them to be. Many and many a night lying out in the hills, watching my fire—like this—I've thought about how it would be, if you were there. How I'd get you to like these hills, and the coyotes talking and the smell of smoke in your hair—you know, foolish stuff."

"I do love the hills," she said.

He shook his head. "This isn't it. This isn't right. You ought to be able to lie by your fire and smell pine timber. And that crick out there ought to have water running in it. You sit and listen to running water, and pretty soon you get to hear voices in it; sometimes you lie awake for hours trying to get what they say. But what's more to the point, there's likewise trout in the water. There ought to be a nice pan of trout frying, here on the fire."

"You fit with things like that, you know. As if you were made out of them."

He said, "A half hour's rest in the rocks, with a long, long walk ahead—this is about as close as people get to the way they want things, I suppose."

"It's my fault, Billy. If I hadn't been so stubborn you wouldn't have lost your horse; you'd have gone on through."

"Shucks, now!"

She was silent, and they sat looking into the fire. The little flickering flame was a slow magic, and the long horseless drag that separated them from the 94 was helping it—drawing them together, shutting the rest of the world away. The smell of autumn was cool and clean in the air, across the dry sage; and the red-gold moon faintly mellowed the chill of darkness on the gaunt hills, so that they sat here in unreality, as if in a dream.

"Some places," he said, "they call that a harvest moon; the Indians call it the hunting moon, and they used to make smoke-medicines by it."

"What do *you* call it?"

"Well—sometimes we call it a coyote moon. Because it puts a kind of singing craze on the coyotes. They gather around on hill tops, seems like, and sing their hearts out, as if it drove them wild crazy, some way. Listen."

Far off, so faint a whisper that it seemed half imagined, they could hear now a queer high crooning, full of an interwoven yapping and trilling, like nothing else on earth.

"It sounds," Marian said, "as if there were forty or

fifty of them—sitting somewhere on a mountain in a ring."

"Two," he told her. "They pair off this time of year."

"Two," she repeated. "Then that's why there's something more than madness in that singing."

He knew that they should be starting the long return, but he could not bring himself to say so. The thing that had brought them together again—the disaster to Horse Dunn and the 94—had nearly run its course. And he knew that it was a good thing for him that it had. Already he had lived under the same roof with Marian too long for his own good. He no longer had any hope that he could forget her; she would always be in the back of his mind some place, waiting to come real and close to him in his dreams.

He supposed he would have to learn to live with those dreams. To sit with her now, far out and alone beside the little fire was itself an unreal and precious thing, now that he no longer fought against it. A quiet peace had come upon this place; or something as near peace as he ever knew any more. She was very near to him, so near that though their shoulders did not touch, it seemed to him that he could feel her warmth; and her hair, with the fire-light in it, was a warm smoky mist, shot with gold, clouding his eyes.

They sat for a long time listening to the faint coyote song and the little popping of the fire. Once, as they sat quiet, he heard far off a thing he did not understand. It was so distant and so muffled that he could not at once decide whether it could have been the fall of a rock from a high place, or had been the report of a gun far away up the canyon, smothered by close walls and the drift of the air. He glanced at Marian to see if she had noticed it, and saw that she had not.

Marian looked at him, the firelight pooling long shadows under the lashes of her steady eyes. "I just thought of something."

"What was it?"

"This—isn't it kind of funny?—this is exactly the situation we were speaking of the other day."

He was puzzled. "When was this?"

"In Inspiration."

For a moment he didn't get it. Then it came back to him in a rush—the blast of sun upon the dusty street, the atmosphere of silent, waiting hostility, the groups of spurred and booted men in doorways, watching without seeming to watch; and he had stood talking to Marian across the door of a car, not thinking about what was ahead.

" 'If you and I were set afoot,' " she quoted, " 'some place far off in the mountains at night, with only one blanket between us—' "

He was resting perfectly still on one elbow, looking at the fire; but he could feel her eyes, so near his face, watching him under her lashes. And behind her eyes he supposed she was laughing at him.

"I was right," she said. "You didn't know it then, but you can see it now. You see—it seems a good deal different, now that we're really here."

"Does it?" he said without expression. He got up with a sort of stiff, slow leisure, for the little fire was burning low. He went beyond the fire, squatted on one heel beside it, and fed it pieces of stick.

"You see, I know you, Billy. Sometimes I think I know you better than I know myself." Her eyes wavered and drifted out toward the low young stars. "I can remember when I was afraid of you. If we had been out here then—two years ago—I would have wanted

156

nothing so much as to get back among other people. That's all gone, now."

He looked at her. She had never seemed more lovely, more human, more elementally desirable than she looked now, a tired girl in cow-country work clothes, slim and lazy, relaxed by the little fire as if she had never known any other resting place in her life. Her face was quiet, almost grave; but though her eyes looked drowsy there was a little gleam in them that did not come from the flame in front: a small provocative glimmer of fire within, which he had seen in her eyes only two or three times in his life—and never before the last two or three days.

Their eyes met and held, his steady and masked within, hers seeming to laugh at him a little, half veiled by her lashes.

"I said," she reminded him, "that if we were—in a situation like this, there wouldn't be anything for me to worry about, nothing at all. And you said, if I thought that I was a fool. Well, you see—" she met his eyes again—"I win."

Still her eyes held, and he could not understand why hers did not drop. "I can't believe, hardly," he said, "that you have any idea what sort of thing you're talking about."

She smiled. "You think I don't? That's because western men are certainly the most conventional people in the world."

Suddenly he angered. He had not brought her here of his own will, nor set them afoot, nor wished to rest here with her. He would not even have been on her range, or within a day's ride of it, if her interests had not drawn him in and held him. She had made her decisions in regard to him long ago, and to change them he had spent

157

his every resource without any effect. And now, at the last—it amused her to torment him. It seemed to him that there was a capricious she-devil in that girl—perhaps in all women, given opportunity.

"You see, I know you," she was saying again.

The masks behind his eyes dropped away, and though his face hardly changed his eyes reddened, seeming to smoke with the angry fire that came up behind. She herself had lighted that fire, long ago. It was a fire that had driven him relentlessly, making him rich; it could have made him work for her all her life—or it could break him again, and drive him up and down the world. Suddenly he did not know whether he loved or hated this girl.

"I'll give you the same answer I gave you in Inspiration," he said, his words almost inaudible, even against the stillness of the night. "If you think that, you're a little fool."

Still she met his eyes, so long, so steadily, so knowingly that he wondered for an instant what was happening, was going to happen, there under the coyote moon.

Then he saw her face change, so that she was suddenly pale, and the unreadable light in her eyes went out, and she was like a little girl. Abruptly she pressed her face hard into her hands.

He made his voice as hard and cold as the rocks that hung over them. "Now what?"

She answered in a muffled voice, "I was wrong—I *am* afraid. I—I fail every one . . ." She lifted her head and glanced about her, as if she were seeing this place for the first time. A black shape lay beside the empty dust of the stream, like a great black bottle overturned—the carcass of Marian's dead horse. Suddenly the girl turned sideways, and dropped her head in her arms upon the blanket. She began to cry, terribly, silently except for the choke of her breath.

He sat down against a rock and waited. The gaunt, dead rock-hills leaned over them sadly cold and silent, blackened by the twisted ghost shapes of the parched brush. And the coyote moon was pale and old, no longer golden, but greenish, like phosphorus rubbed on a dead and frozen face.

Once she said, "But it's your fault, too—that I fail—your fault as much as my own."

His answer was perfectly honest. "I don't know what you mean."

CHAPTER TWENTY-TWO

It was impossible for him to sit waiting for her weeping to stop, while her slim body shook convulsively with her effort to suppress it, and her breath jerked uncontrollably in her throat. Her tumbled hair made her seem a child; he had never seen her look so small, so fragilely made. And he thought he had never in his life seen anything so pitifully in need of comforting.

He swore under his breath and got to his feet. For a few moments he stood over her, watching the movement of the firelight in her hair. He could hardly prevent himself from touching her; almost he stooped and picked her up in his arms. But he was telling himself that that was the thing she wanted.

He walked out a little way into the dark, and stood listening to the night silence. He was still worrying about the distant muffled sound of concussion which he

159

had heard. It seemed to him now that what he had heard was unquestionably the sound of a gun—perhaps a gun fired near the forgotten miner's shanty at the upper end of the gulch; but what he could not imagine was who could have fired it. He had assumed that it was Lon Magoon who had killed Marian's pony; but now he saw that something was wrong. If Magoon had fired upon Marian Dunn and killed her horse he would not have gone to the cabin at the head of the gulch, but would have put long country between himself and them. Therefore two men, not one, must be prowling these hills. He thought of Coffee's theory that there had been a third man at Short Crick—and was worse puzzled than before.

He was trying to guess who the second man could be. Vaguely he was thinking of the green eyes of Rufe Deane, watching Marian as she testified against the Bender faction at the Inspiration hearing. He knew that there was nothing behind the eyes of that embittered man which would prevent his firing upon the girl—if a reason for such an act could be conceived. But still he could think of no explanation for the firing of that other distant gun.

Abruptly he turned and went back to the fire. Marian was sitting up, trying to press the redness from her eyes; she seemed steady again. "Sorry," she said.

"I've got to go on up the canyon," he told her.

"I thought you said Magoon wouldn't stop there, now."

He told her, shortly, of the distant report of the gun.

"But who could it be?"

"I don't know. But—I've got to go up and see."

"I'm ready to start," Marian said.

"Ready—?"

"I'm going to go where you go."

He considered a moment. She looked tired, and there was a long hour of rough travel between them and the hidden cabin. But he supposed she would not want to try to wander back through the dark alone; nor could he, against her will, leave her to imagine horrors in the dark. The hard twist of his mouth turned a shade more grim.

"Very well," he said. "But you're going to be a little tired before the night's over, I'm afraid."

"I don't care anything about that."

To a tired rider a trail can unroll interminably ahead; much worse is a trail on foot, forever upward into increasing dark. To a walker accustomed to the saddle one mile seems ten. It could not have been more than three miles to the ancient shack at the head of the gulch, but they climbed continually; and the twist of the dry stream lengthened the miles. He knew that often Marian was trying to conceal from him the laboring of her breath in the high air. It must have seemed to the girl that she plodded and stumbled all night long through that uphill sand, while Wheeler's long stride led out relentlessly. She could not know how much he slowed his pace for her.

The broad canyon narrowed and steepened until it was a twisting gorge between vast black walls. The going became steeper, and the sand shelves ended; the dead stream was an interminable staircase of ledges and tumbles of rock. They had traveled an interminable time before Wheeler whispered to her, "We've got to be quieter now." And still they went on, climbing a long way.

He was moving slowly and very cautiously when at last he turned off and worked his way up a gravelly slide of stone; then forward through twisting juniper that clung to the steep land. He stopped, gripped her shoulders, thrust her downward to her knees.

"What—"

He stopped her whisper with a quick hand over her mouth; but directly ahead, not a dozen paces away, she was answered by the sudden long snort of a pony. He was peering through the juniper; her eyes followed his, straining in the canyon's black shadows. What he was looking at took form in the darkness, and without moving seemed to appear suddenly all at once. With a shock she saw that they were not fifteen steps away from a small ruined shanty set hard against an overhanging wall of stone.

The shack at the head of the gulch was windowless, and its door was open into blackness. Beside it, tied some yards apart, were the horse which had snorted, and a second animal that might have been either a horse or a mule.

Wheeler backed away, drawing her after him, foot by foot. Fifty yards away in the shelter of the rocks he made her sit down. No sound came from above except the uneasy shifting of the ponies' feet; and Wheeler permitted himself a deep breath of relief. She could hardly hear his whisper in the dark: "I didn't remember it was so close."

"Is he there?"

"Someone's there, or the horses would be gone. Wait here."

Slowly Wheeler made his way upward again over the rocks, through the juniper scrub. Walking upright, but very quietly, he circled and approached along the rock wall, until his hands found the side of the cabin itself. He pressed an ear against the rough timber, and listened

162

for long minutes. But he could hear nothing, not even the drawing of a breath.

He took out his knife and cut a plume of brush. Standing close against the corner of the cabin he struck a match and set the brush aflame. He was holding his breath as he did that If the man he sought was playing the old Indian trick of moving away a few yards from his camp to sleep in the open, then the striking of a light here at the cabin end would be a good signal for gunfire. But the dry oily, brush blazed up quickly in his hands, blinding him with its sudden light, and nothing happened. Instantly he swung an arm around the corner of the cabin and threw the lighted brush through the open door.

Crouching low, he moved ten paces from the cabin and circled slowly, watching the lighted doorway. He could see the blazing brush on the cabin's floor of hard-packed earth, and no hand moved to put it out. Behind the flame the cabin's interior was barren; he made out an ancient brush jacket hung against the wall, the three-legged ruin of a crude table, the black shadow of a bunk. Someone was here—should be here; but if the fugitive had been in the cabin he would have thrown a blanket over that torch by now. Wheeler wondered if the man was behind him, or drawing a bead on him from above.

Then as he circled a high-heeled boot came into view upon the cabin floor. That boot was unnatural; it was lying on its side, yet not on its side—tilted up a little upon its toe. When he saw that, something turned over inside Wheeler, for he knew what was in the cabin. He straightened up and walked to the door, stepped inside quickly and flattened himself against a wall.

The flickering flame of the brush was lower now, but

by what was left of its light he was looking, for the first time in his life, at the face of Lon Magoon. Although he had never seen Magoon before he was sure at once who this man had been. The small stature and pinched build of the cow thief, "like a grasshopper, or a flea," was partial identification; and there were other reasons to believe that this was he. Magoon had fallen forward; there was a rifle under him, and it was at the cock. But it was not in his hands, for his arms were folded tight against his body. And his face was turned to the side, a pinched, almost wizened face, frowsy with a patchy grey beard of three weeks' growth.

The brush torch wavered and went out with a sudden odor of smoke. Wheeler found another match, struck it, and stepped forward to see how this man had died. But even before he turned the cow thief over he knew that Lon Magoon had died by shotgun, as had Cayuse Cayetano and Bob Flagg.

CHAPTER TWENTY-THREE

THE 94, LIFELESS AND SILENT UNDER THE LOW-swinging moon, appeared deserted as Marian Dunn and Billy Wheeler trotted in, riding the horse and the mule they had found at Magoon's cabin. "You go on in, Marian. I'll take care of your horse."

Marian said in a small voice, "Is everyone gone from here?"

No need to remind her that the sheriff must certainly have come and gone, and taken Horse Dunn with him, by now. "It must be after midnight," he said. "Whoever is here must have turned in."

She walked off toward the silent house. It would not

have surprised him if they had found themselves entirely alone; but by the time he had finished tossing hay to their animals he heard the murmur of voices, and, following Marian, he found her talking to Old Man Coffee. The old lion hunter sat angularly on a low step, the coal of his pipe glowing and dying out again at slow intervals.

"Marian tells me you caught up with Lon Magoon."

"We found him, all right."

"How was he killed?"

"With a shotgun; same as the rest."

"I was kind of looking for that," Coffee said. "Lucky, though, that you stumbled onto it so quick."

Marian sat down on the step beside Old Man Coffee. "Why were you looking for it?" she demanded.

"Well—" Coffee paused and seemed to consider—"kind of hard to say. One thing, I've been to Pahranagat since I seen you. I didn't tell you I was going there, but I had a kind of hunch, and so I went. And I got trace of Bob Flagg there at Pahranagat. Seems like he was coming to the 94 by kind of a back way; and at Pahranagat he run into Lon Magoon. He bought or borried a cheap horse and a worn out saddle from Magoon, and they rode out of Pahranagat together. Begins to look like Lon Magoon was a witness to the killing of Bob Flagg."

"But how do you know," Marian said, "that Magoon himself didn't kill Flagg?"

"Well—these killings being done with a shotgun is kind of unusual; it makes you think the same killer attended to all three. And it's easy to see, too, how Magoon might have been a kind of a distant witness. Suppose Magoon was riding along with Flagg, who didn't know him very well. Pretty soon Magoon sees

165

some local cowman coming toward them. Magoon doesn't want to fall in with any local cowman, on account of the business he's in. He splits off and kind of hovers in the distance. In a case like that, him not getting out of sight soon enough would just be suicide for him. Whoever killed Flagg would figure he had to kill Magoon before he talked."

"Did you see Val Douglas at Pahranagat?"

"No, he wasn't there when I was. But he's been back here, tonight, since I been here. He said Pahranagat was where he was. Well, I don't know; I didn't see him there. And according to him he couldn't get any trace of Bob Flagg."

"Is he here now?"

"He pulled right out again. Nobody's here, but me and that old woman that cooks. She claims the sheriff come in and took Horse Dunn to Inspiration, about an hour before I got here. Tulare Callahan come in with Horse; they was pretty much worried over where you was, Marian. Tulare saddled up again and rode out to see if he could find out where you had went. Later Steve Hurley come in, and he's gone looking for you too. So naturally Val Douglas, he figured he'd have to make as good a showing as anybody did, and he hightailed. So now the whole 94 is out hunting for you—what of 'em isn't in jail."

"Men make me so mad!" Marian declared. "I have a good notion to go riding out looking for them, now just to make the picture of idiocy complete!"

Coffee looked as if he wouldn't put it past her. "Oh, now, I wouldn't go and do that, child."

"Coffee," Billy said, "one other kind of funny thing happened, while we were out. That hombre that shot at Marian the other night—he took another try."

166

"Damn!" said Coffee. "He come close?"

"Killed her horse. I got nervous and let my own pony get loose, and he stampeded. Later we had to come back on mule Magoon had tied up, and a horse he stole from the 94." Old Man Coffee turned slowly and for a few moments studied Marian's face. "Uh huh," he said at last.

There was a silence. "What do you think of it?" Marian said.

"I think," said Coffee, "you better turn in."

Marian rose slowly. "I suppose you're right—I've made enough trouble for one day, haven't I?"

When she was gone Billy Wheeler took her place on the step beside Old Man Coffee. "Well, we're slowly learning a thing or two," he said. "God knows where this thing leads to; but it ought to lead some place pretty soon."

Old Man Coffee knocked out his pipe, refilled it again, and struck a new light. In the flare of the match his bony old face looked more grim and more sardonic than ever. "It ain't going to lead me no place. It's led me far enough. I'm through!"

Wheeler did not argue this. Twice before Coffee had made such hollow threats; he did not believe the old lion hunter would actually withdraw now.

"One thing I didn't tell you about Bob Flagg," Coffee said. "I suppose you got a right to what I know. Well—here's a little item that's a peach! Flagg—he bummed his way into Pahranagat in an empty cow car."

Wheeler was astounded. "You sure must be wrong," he declared. "Why, that sounds crazy! He and Dunn had just sold out the Arizona ranch, at Dunn's order. Dunn's share was the biggest, and of course they couldn't get but part cash; but there was fifty thousand ready mony

167

mixed into the deal. Flagg didn't have any reason for coming in any such way as that!"

"He done it, though. It was right hard for me to find anybody that knew he'd been there at all. Sure seems like Flagg was taking every way he could think of to get to the 94 without being noticed. I thought it was kind of peculiar that Flagg should come by way of Pahranagat, which is kind of like sliding in the back door. Still, that wouldn't mean anything by itself; some of us old guys get used to thinking in terms of saddle work. But this other thing—it's queer."

"Well, you must have mistaken your man!"

"No, I didn't."

Wheeler turned thoughtful, and they were silent for some minutes. A dark and ugly reason for Flagg's peculiar behavior was taking shape. "Coffee," he said slowly, "you see what it means? *Bob Flagg had foreknowledge of his death.* He knew what was ahead of him when he came into the Red Rock."

"Yes," said Old Man Coffee, "it sure appears like he did."

"Do you suppose Lon Magoon could have been a spy, sent to Pahranagat to watch for Bob Flagg?"

"A spy for who?"

"A spy for the men that set out to kill Flagg. We know who the enemies of the 94 are. Link Bender—Pinto Halliday—Rufe Deane—even Sam Caldwell—there isn't a one of them that would have hesitated to shoot a man down, if it meant wiping out the 94. We know that those people, or some of them, got access to Horse Dunn's mail at Inspiration. We can figure they knew that the Arizona outfit was sold, and that Flagg was on the way here with the money—money that the 94 had to have to pull through."

"I had that figured out long ago," Coffee said. "I figured Cayuse Cayetano was the cat's paw for Link Bender. Even after Cayetano was killed, I thought maybe they just killed him so he wouldn't turn state's evidence."

"But you don't think that now?"

"Now," said Coffee, "I don't think."

"Throw out the death of Cayuse," Wheeler suggested. "Say that he was killed simply because he was too hot on the trail. Throw out the death of Magoon—say that he was feared as a distant witness. It turns back to the enemies of the 94."

"Which includes everybody," Coffee snorted.

"Coffee—you've found out something you're holding back!"

Coffee shook his head. "You know everything I know so far as I can think."

"Then you have some way of reading the facts—some way different from what I've got."

"Maybe. I've quit bothering my head about it."

"Hell! You'll never make me think that you're going to pull out of this case and leave it unsolved."

"There's just one thing about this case," Coffee admitted, "that I sure hate to leave mixed up. How come old Rock and me to get mixed up about the trail of the killer horse? I s'pose all the rest of my life—" Old Man Coffee's voice was bitter—"I'll never get away from wondering how come I lost that trail."

"Of course, if I remember rightly," Wheeler reminded him, "you figured out from the way the shot went into the saddle that the man on the so-called killer horse was not the killer."

"That ain't important. The man on the killer horse took and hid the body, anyway. Two men or one—

169

comes to the same thing. Catch one and you catch both."

"You still think the killer's horse was here it the 94 layout after the killing, like old Rock seemed to think?"

Old Man Coffee's answer was a grunt; it might have meant one thing or the other. "You're stalled, son. You got no lead."

"Sure we've got a lead."

"And where is that?"

"Just a minute ago we were talking about the peculiar way Bob Flagg kind of eased into the Red Rock, coming in through the back way, bumming it in a cattle crate. From what we know Bob Flagg had fore-knowledge that somebody was going to make a try for him. Now, *how did Bob Flagg come by that fore-knowledge?*"

Old Man Coffee did not reply. Out by the corrals a hound moaned in its chest; the dog called old Rock awoke by Coffee's feet, raised its head to listen, then blew out a long breath and went back to sleep again.

"Coffee—I'm thinking now that when we find out how Bob Flagg come by that fore-knowledge, we'll have caught our man."

With an impatient movement Old Man Coffee knocked out his pipe again. "You want to know what I think? I think, 'Oh, hell!' You better go on to bed."

Obviously Old Man Coffee was tired of arguing. Wheeler had been trying to lead the old man out, and it had got him nowhere. He rose slowly and stretched. "Guess you're right. Seems like you might need some sleep, too."

"Slept all the way from Pahranagat, on the top of my mule. I'll get plenty rest sitting right here with my pipe." He added irascibly, "Or I will if the everlasting talky-talk dries up."

"Looks like it might slack off some," Wheeler grinned. He went in, fumbled his way through the dark house to his room, flung his gun belt on the floor, and lighted his lamp.

CHAPTER TWENTY-FOUR

IT WAS VERY LATE. WITHOUT CHECKING THE HOUR, HE knew that morning could not be far off; and he had supposed that Marian was asleep. She had ridden a long way, not to count that long climb of theirs through the dark. In her own way she outlasted the leathery strength of men and horses—and came through clear-eyed and light-footed, apparently untouched. But she seemed so fragilely made that he always underestimated the young strength of her vitality.

So, he was thinking of her as asleep, as he now sat down on the edge of his bunk and rolled a cigarette. His long-boned frame rested relaxed, but he did not look tired. All his life had been spent in the saddle, simply for the reason that the dry country has few roads—few places for roads to go—and the horse is the only means of cross country transportation across mountain ranges and sand dunes and the vast gulch-cut plains. Ten thousand miles in the saddle had hardened him until he was made of braided leather, and no less enduring than the runty, unkillable range ponies. A few more miles on the horse trails and a few nights short of sleep could not tire him now. His leanly-muscled face was as awake as ever, and his grey eyes, made to look lighter than they were by his wind-burned and weather-leathered skin, were as clear as they had been when he arrived at the

94. He let his cigarette trail from a corner of his mouth, rested his chin on one hand; and, squinting through the thin upward-moving line of smoke, considered his next moves.

He must travel—that was certain. What could be done here was done—the finding of Bob Flagg and Lon Magoon. He must trace Bob Flagg back to his sources, back through Flagstaff, perhaps to the sold-out Arizona ranch itself, seeking the truth about that strange fore-knowledge of Flagg's; for he was certain that Flagg had shown more than a premonition of his death.

And he must find time to run down the 94 debts, seeking ways to avert its bankruptcy, at least for a time. He was wondering how far he dared go against Dunn's order that no penny of Wheeler money should ever be chanced in the 94. Dunn would be game to split the works wide open, if he didn't like the way salvation had been obtained. It was up to Wheeler to find ways to get around that, taking care that the girl would never guess any obligation to him. That last was what Dunn feared most.

But though his mind was laying out routes and plans far outside of the Red Rock country, he was somehow not surprised as Marian now came and joined him here. To think about any phase of this killing case, or of the imminent ruin of Horse Dunn's cow kingdom, was to think about her. After all, the 94 was her brand, and her future was interlaced with its future. So now as he looked up at the sound of her light quick step it seemed a natural, somehow expected thing to see her standing there in his door.

"This is a lonely night," she said. "Nothing anywhere in this night intends to sleep."

"I guess that's so. But it's near morning now."

Without high heels and with her hair light and loose about her shoulders she should have looked smaller, but she did not. He thought he had never seen her so slimly tall, so gravely steady. Perhaps that was partly the effect of what she wore. Because he had never seen her dressed as she was now, he had a sudden sense of how little he knew her, after all; just as he did not know what she wore when she slept, how could he know what went on in her mind when she was alone—or ever?

What she was really wearing were pajamas, but their black silk was cut like a Russian smock, with a high close collar of soft black silk about her throat, and close cuffs at her wrists, so that standing against the dark she was all a part of the dark, except for the bright ivory of her face and hands and the loose shimmer of her hair. About this costume, which was strange to him, there was a barbaric dignity, as if it were not something to sleep in at all, but the ceremonial dress of some forgotten priestess. It was strange to see this vision here, standing beside a spare saddle that had been flung on the floor under a tangle of bridles on a wooden peg. Everything around her was cow country, but she—she was something else, something lovely from beyond the hills—a daughter of two worlds.

She came and sat beside him on the bunk. "Did you find out anything more from Old Man Coffee? I thought you'd get more out of him if I left you alone."

"Not very much. Old Man Coffee's been a disappointment to me in a way. Sometimes I think he doesn't know anything about it."

"I wonder."

"Marian, what are you going to do?"

"What is there for me to do? One of two things—stay here or go to Inspiration to be near Horse. Of course, he

173

ought to be out of there in a few days."

"I wouldn't count on that, Marian. They can't make a case against him—not even the beginnings of a case. They know that. But what they want to do—and can do—is to tie up the 94 finances by making the case look as ugly as possible. They'll point out that Dunn was the main one who would be expecting Flagg there and probably make Flagg's share of the money the motive. Of course that's ridiculous. But for their purpose, all they need to do is to raise the question and then cause a delay in clearing it up."

Her eyes were on distance beyond the walls—smoky eyes, drowsy, even misty on the surface—but behind them was that continuing deep glow of slumbering fire, the smouldering light of a great reserve vitality.

"I'd go east now, if I were you," he told her. "We'll fight this thing out, and save out of it what we can—you can count on that. But—this isn't a good place for you any more. There won't be anyone here, except a couple of cow hands to keep an eye on things. And it would drive Horse crazy to have you in; that hornets' nest in Inspiration."

"But you—?"

"I'll be gone. I have to back-track Bob Flagg a little further. I'll have to go to Flagstaff; then maybe down-country. God knows how long I'll be gone. It looks like a dim, crooked trail."

She considered this. "When are you leaving?"

"Now—before daylight. I'll send a note to Horse. I don't even dare see him in Inspiration, for fear they'll hold me there on some trumped—up charge."

They were silent again. Through the window came to them a cool, fragrantly clean breeze from the uplands, with a fall tang in it that promised frosts before long. He

174

suddenly thought she might be cold. There was a clean Navajo blanket on his bed, and he put this about her shoulders. She smiled faintly, but did not look at him or move.

She said, "It will be queer and lonely here, with you gone."

"But you'll be leaving too."

She shook her head, her eyes far away. "I'm through with hovering on the outskirts of my own life."

For a moment he wondered what provision he could make for her safety here. He no longer doubted that what she determined to do she would do, and could not be dissuaded from. He thought of consigning her safety to Old Man Coffee, or to the cowboys now searching the hills for her; but he was deeply concerned.

"Sometimes I think," Marian said, "that the answer to everything is to be found right here—here at the 94— and no place else."

He nodded moodily. "A man ought to be able to figure it out, if he was smart."

"There isn't anything more you could follow up, here? When time is so important—"

"There's one lone, slim possibility," he said.

"In heaven's name, what is it?"

"There's one thing in this case that I can't swallow. It stands out above everything else—one unbelievable thing that couldn't possibly happen. I'm thinking of those two shots that have been thrown at—you."

She was silent, and after a moment or two he went on. "Somehow those shots at you are mixed up with these other shootings; it would be too big a coincidence if the shots at you and the killing of the men were separate, yet happening at the same time."

"I can see that, all right."

175

"But the shots at you eliminate nearly every suspect we have. Take Val Douglas. He hasn't proved very dependable, Marian. Three times now he's been caught in lies as to where he was. Even just now, when he was sent to Pahranagat to check up Bob Flagg, it seems from what Coffee says that he didn't even go near there. Sometimes I've suspected Val. Even if he didn't kill Flagg to rob him, still he might have killed him by mistake, thinking it was somebody else. But one thing is certainly plain—Val Douglas would never fire on you.

"No," Marian said, "Val could never do that."

"Or take Link Bender—a hard, bitter, violent man. Once he was boss of all this range, until Horse Dunn took hold. Link Bender might go to any length to put down the 94. But he controls this kid sheriff, and through the sheriff he's bearing down on the 94 through this killing; and he's getting away with it. His whole way of attack is orderly and thought out. He wouldn't try any such crazy thing as shooting a girl."

"It's pretty hard to see in what way I could stand between Link Bender and his plans.

"The same thing applies to Pinto Halliday; he's a shifty crook, but he isn't crazy. Sam Caldwell is another that it doesn't fit in with."

"The thing just won't fit together, will it?"

"Marian, it's in my mind that I know who killed Bob Flagg."

"Billy! If you know that—"

"There's one man in that Inspiration crowd that is too savage bitter to wait for Link Bender's plan to pan out. That man is Rufe Deane. Rufe Deane blames Horse for the death of his son, years ago."

"Yes," Marian said, "I've thought of him."

"Rufe Deane tried to raise a mob in Inspiration to see

176

that the 94 people never got away from there. If he had started in time, there'd have been a lynching before midnight. He threw down his deputy's badge because he thought the sheriff was going too easy with Horse. And when you testified for me at the hearing—Rufe Deane was looking at you like a wolf waiting. Marian, I believe Rufe Deane is one man that's crazy enough and bitter enough to try to kill you—to get back at Horse for the death of young Deane."

"Billy, if you're right—if you can prove that—"

"That's just the trouble. Suppose I'm right—Rufe Deane did it. We're no better off than we were in the beginning. You see, Marian, there's two parts to these killing cases. One thing is to find out who did it and why. The other thing is to prove it and get a conviction. I haven't one single thing to show against Rufe Deane; and until I can show evidence, it won't matter how sure I may be in my mind."

When he looked at her it was past his power to imagine how Rufe Deane or anyone else could ever look down the sights of a gun at Marian Dunn; she was so gently and sweet made, so precious in his eyes. He didn't believe in Horse Dunn's creed of gun justice, for he thought that the use of violence outside the law was a costly thing, defeating its own purpose in the end. But he knew that if ever he faced Rufe Deane with anything like a decent proof in his hands, he would destroy the killer as he would destroy a sidewinder or a vinegaroon.

"I'll never be able to believe in God's world that anyone would set out to hurt you," he said. "Yet—somebody has tried. What naturally comes to mind is that somebody, some enemy of Horse Dunn, has gone out of his head. But—hard as it is to believe, there is one other possibility we have to take account of—that without knowing it you've heard something, or seen something, which would give away the Short Creek killer—if you remembered it, and recognized it for what it was."

She said, "I've thought of that."

"Marian, if you can remember seeing anything—a rider in the distance—some horse coming home at a strange time—one of the guns missing from its rack here in the house—even an empty shell that you thought nothing of—that one thing might give us the answer!"

"I've racked my brain over and over; but I can't think of anything, Billy."

"Not even a chance word, overheard somewhere—"

She shook her head. "Billy, I just can't remember anything that would answer the purpose at all." She pressed her palms against her eyes for a moment; then lifted her head sharply shaking out her loose hair. "It's no use. This isn't the first time I've tried to remember; I've been trying hard for two days."

"I thought it would most likely be hopeless," he admitted. "Well—I'll have to go to Flagstaff."

"I know. I've seen that coming. I'm ready to stay here alone; without you or my uncle, I mean."

"Marian, if I could get you to pull out of here, until this is over—"

"This is my outfit, Billy. It shouldn't be my outfit; it should be my mother's, or Horse Dunn's. But nothing can make Horse see that. And I see now that if you're going to run cattle on a big scale out in this country, you sometimes have to be willing to fight for your range."

He stared at her, marveling. The girl who was talking to him now was not the girl he had known two years ago, she was not even the girl he had known at the beginning of the week. It was as if some false outer

178

cloaking of ideas and habits, put upon her by her mother's seaboard world, had suddenly fallen away, leaving her revealed as what she was—a daughter of the dry land. Under the pressure of the dark days and unquiet nights since the killing of Bob Flagg she had come nearer to him, becoming one of his own people.

"Seems to me," he said, "that's a whole lot different from what you were saying just a little while ago."

"I wasn't able to believe my own eyes, I guess. I wasn't able to get over the 'settled-up' idea that eastern people have. Nobody but westerners will ever be able to understand our dry land. They'll never believe that a country can be over-settled—and yet have nothing in it but coyotes and jackrabbits and half a dozen poor cows to the mile."

He noticed that she called it "our dry land," now.

"And so—?"

"I'm going to stay with my brand, until there isn't one bit of the 94 left. After all, I'm my father's daughter. This country is part of me, bred in."

"I know how you feel," he said slowly. "But—it isn't as if you really do anything here, now."

"I'll be able to keep you informed of what's happening here, at least. I hardly think Val Douglas would take much interest in that, left to himself. But it isn't that. It's simply—I can't always run away from everything. I've run away from too many things, and sometimes afterward I've been sorry."

He could understand that, but it surprised him to find her looking at things in that way. He had to respect her for it, but it didn't make the set-up any easier for him. "I suppose there isn't anything I can do," he admitted regretfully. "You've already shown me that when you set out to do a thing, you'll do it in spite of all hell and

179

the drought."

"Wouldn't you rather have me that way?"

"I don't know as I could ever bring myself to want you any different than you are."

He made a cigarette, and lit it, and gloomily studied its smoke. He was thinking that it was pretty near too much to ask of a man to go off on a long trail, the way things were here, and leave this child—

Suddenly he realized that this girl in black silk and bright Navajo wool was not any longer a child. He had not known that he had always before seen her as a child, until now he saw her as something else. Her face had a color that was like a child's color, clear and lovely, but its contour no longer suggested a little girl. It was a quiet face, thoughtful and awake, and somehow competent looking; and her eyes, looking into that distance beyond the walls, were looking into the future—understandingly, even somberly, but unafraid.

He wondered why he had not realized before how changed she was. Every movement she made, every pose she took, was different from what he had seen in the girl he had made love to two years before. Two years ago Marian Dunn would not have been able to lounge relaxed upon his bunk in pajamas and an Indian blanket, thinking about the factors of range war, and the business affairs of men; she would have been nervously conscious then of the fact that the man she was with loved her—would have worried about what he would do or say.

This girl did not worry, but steadily faced the situation in which they found themselves.

He looked away from her, unable any longer to think of murder clues or cow mortgages while she was in his eyes. He fixed his gaze upon his thrown-down gunbelt and tried to think of what he must do. Bitterly he was blaming himself that he could not see through this killing case; for he had a persistent hunch that everything necessary for solution was in his hands. He blamed only himself that he must now take a long trail to discover what might be obvious, here and now, to a more brilliant deduction.

He tried to set his mind to the factors he had discussed with Coffee, in one more supreme effort to short-cut the case, but his mind would not work for him. Even with his eyes upon a saddle or a gun he could still see nothing but the girl—every glint of light in the loose bush of her hair, the slim cordings of a wrist, the resting look of a hand that lay palm up upon the blanket.

Impossible not to wonder if things between them might not have been different had he never known her two years before at all, but could have started over again now, to win her in a new way. Then it occurred to him that it was a waste of time to be looking at a gun or a saddle blanket, trying to think, when he might be looking at her. Perhaps it would be a long time before he would see her again; perhaps he would never see her again at all.

So now he let murder and cows and money slide into the lost shadows, and he turned to her; and as he did so he found that her eyes were on his face. They looked at each other steadily, while the moments passed. If he had held her eyes so long two years ago she would have flushed and looked away, but she did not look away now. Her eyes looked lazy, but not sleepy; they were as darkly blue as a night sky, but he found them unreadable at first. Then after a moment or two he recognized that she was not thinking about murder clues.

All at once he knew that there was no barrier between them any more at all, and had not been any for a long time, except the barrier put there by his old defeat. And he knew now that he had never failed at all, but that the years had worked for him in ways he would not have guessed.

He said slowly, "I was the one who was a fool."

He never knew what move he made that brought her into his arms. With the barrier gone from between them at last they found themselves in each other's arms as naturally, as unhurriedly, as inevitably as the dry land takes up the rare rains; and his heart lifted up like the April grass of the dry ranges, when the snow-lock melts off and is forgotten as if it had never been. His hungry mouth found an answering quiver in her lips; and for a while, under the spell of the gentle warmth that he had thought would never be his, he no longer worried about what might happen to the cow kingdom of Horse Dunn.

Presently she said, "Two years ago it was my fault. But last night in the hills it was yours. If you had only put your hands on me then—but you had to stand with a face like granite, and eyes like death in the foothills—"

"I know that—now."

"I don't know how I'm going to let you go. So many things—anything—can happen before we're together again."

"But we have this hour, now."

"Nothing can ever rob us of that!"

Each was seeing a person he had never seen before. He was still whipcord and braided leather, the saddle man who could hold his own in the upheaval of markets and the shifting games of the financiers; but all the barbed and dour hardness of him was gone, so that in the arms of this girl it was as if he were reborn. And in the girl the hidden steel of the will he had not been able to bend seemed melted, and the curve of her body within his arm was a surrender without reserve.

They did not know how long they lay together on the bunk that for the time was not his, but theirs, in that lonely and deserted house; and he learned here that she was neither east nor west, but all woman, more woman than he could have suspected or known. A harsh, taut strain that had held them for days seemed to slacken and go out of the night, as if guns and cattle were unimportant things; and in that hour that was theirs alone, one bitterness went out of the world forever. It was not a surprise, but a consummation, when presently he found that she was asleep.

He picked her up and carried her to her own room, and put her in her own bed; and she smiled faintly in her sleep as he kissed her eyes. Then he walked out of the house, by a different door than the one where Coffee sat, and stood listening to the still night.

Then, while his mind was entirely away from hatred and violence for the first time in a week, something in the back of his mind found the answer, and all in a moment he saw through the tangle that had roped the 94. He knew suddenly not only who had killed Flagg at Short Creek, but why Flagg had had more than a hunch that he was riding into death; he knew why Marian had been fired on; and he knew how he could prove, inevitably and inescapably, who had killed Bob Flagg—and the taut strain of range war came back into the night, turning him cold.

CHAPTER TWENTY-FIVE

WHEELER WALKED AROUND THE HOUSE TO WHERE OLD Man Coffee still sat. As far as the naked eye could observe Old Man Coffee had not changed his position; he could sit like a rock or an Indian hours on end, as if this were his natural way of living out his life. Wheeler sat down slowly and stiffly on the step beside the old man; he ran his hands over his face, shook his head like a fighter trying to clear away the effects of a killing right cross.

Coffee did not speak and for a little while Wheeler also sat silent, trying to compute how much he wished to say. "Coffee," he said at last, "I see it. I see it all."

Coffee took his pipe out of his mouth and looked at Wheeler. "All what?"

"I know who fired on Marian."

"Hell, son, you had that figured out last time I seen you, two hours ago." Coffee glanced at the stars which he used as a clock. "Two hours and fifteen minutes," he corrected himself.

"I had the wrong reason," Wheeler said; "this time I know. And knowing that, I know why Bob Flagg had fore-notice that he was near his end. And I can prove it all."

Old Man Coffee started to say, "You sound like you was full of—" but he hesitated and studied Billy Wheeler sidelong through the thin dark. "Answer me one thing, son," he said at last. "What was the thing that showed you the killer trail?"

"It was two things, Coffee," Wheeler said; "not one. Two kind of trivial-looking things, that I knew and then

184

forgot. But as soon as I saw the meaning of one of them, right away I saw the meaning of the other. Like as if the two clues were tied together by the neck. Coffee, Marian doesn't know a thing in the world about this. But the first thing that come to me was something I remembered that she said. You remember after—"

"Stop," said Old Man Coffee.

So sharply had the old man commanded him that Wheeler at first thought Coffee was listening to some distant sound. "What's the matter?"

"I've heard enough."

"Then," said Billy Wheeler, "you know the answer too?"

"I've kind of suspected it these many days. I didn't know for sure until today."

"Do you think anyone else knows?"

"Son, I'm virtually certain that no one in the world knows but you and me."

"You must have come at it differently than I did, Coffee."

"Different than you," Coffee agreed. "God knows how you come at it. I don't want to know. In a minute now I'm going to say no more. But nobody else in the Red Rock could have found it out except maybe Cayuse Cayetano—and he's dead."

They sat silent for a little time. "What's the next move?" Wheeler presently asked.

"Until you spoke," Coffee said, "I knew what my next move was going to be. My next move was going to be *out*. But now that you've come onto the right trail, I guess maybe it's kind of up to me to stand by a little while, until I see what you do."

Something in Old Man Coffee's voice bothered Wheeler. "You mean we're not working together, then?"

"Seems like we might not be, son. I'm an old man; and I long ago learned that sometimes it's a good idea to leave sleeping dogs lie."

"You mean, you'd have been willing to pull out of this case and leave it unsolved forever?"

Old Man Coffee drew half a dozen slow puffs on his pipe before he answered. "The first murder case I worked on," he said at last, "was a long time ago. Sometimes I think that one case was the misfortune of my life. Because it gave me a kind of a reputation in a small way, so that ever since then I've been called in on such, from time to time, over and over again. Man hunting isn't a pretty job, Billy, nor anything a man would care to turn his hand to more than once, if he could get out of it. But I've always worked hard and honestly on any case where I once set my hand. And now that I'm old I figure to keep one right to myself—the right to keep my mouth shut if I can't see where clearing up a mystery will serve no proper end. Take this case, here. Do you think that solving this crime can possibly come under the head of helping any living person, or preserving the peace? You know better than that. You know as well as I do that the minute the answer is made known the guns will crack out, and good boys that's got nothing to do with either side will be throwing lead into each other's guts. And there won't be anything but blood and gunsmoke come out of your damn solution."

"You think Horse Dunn will take to the guns?"

"Of course he'll take to the guns! You know him well enough to know that. The guns will be talking before ever the thing is proved."

"The proof ought to be easy enough."

186

"I got no doubt of that. I see at least one way of proof and maybe you see more. But what I'm telling you is this, son—think what you're doing before you raise this lid. Don't raise it unless you think you'd rather see what will come of it, in place of what we already got."

The moon was gone, and they sat in the chill blackness before dawn; but it seemed to Wheeler that the night was no darker than his mood. "I thought of all that," he said. "I thought of all that the moment it come to me. And first off, I thought like you. But now—I'm not so sure. Sometimes it seems like there's something unsound at the bottom of any plan that calls for just hiding our heads."

"Then I'll give you your answer," said Old Man Coffee abruptly. "I'll give you the whole thing, once and for all, in two words. *Think of the girl.*" He took a couple of drags on his pipe. "Forget Horse Dunn, and the cattle, and the money, and the range. Forget even the good fighting boys, here on the 94—Tulare and Steve Hurley and Val Douglas—they'll fight while they can hold up their guns. And Gil Baker, he'll be in it if he has to drag a broken leg into the street. But forget all them. And think what this here head-on smash between the 94 and all of the rest of the range is going to mean to the girl."

Wheeler sat silent for a long time. At last, needing to be alone, he got up and walked off into the dark, leaving Old Man Coffee with the darkness and his pipe. He went out and he sat on the corrals, and he was thinking about Horse Dunn and the cow kingdom of the 94; but mostly he was thinking about the girl who had at last taken him to her heart, now at the end. He could never think about anything any more except in terms of its effect upon her.

He had an hour to come to his decision there before the first pale, reddish light of the dawn showed at the edge of the world; and it was the hardest hour of his life, because he knew that he held in his hands the future of them all. More than once he turned to Coffee's easier way. But as a grey light began to come slowly across the 94 he thought he knew what he must do.

He went in and rapped on Marian's door; and when she called to him sleepily he went in and stood beside her. "You and I are going to Inspiration," he told her.

CHAPTER TWENTY-SIX

THE EARLY SUN WAS UPON THE BROAD MAIN STREET OF Inspiration as Billy Wheeler drove Horse Dunn's touring car into the little cow town. Old Man Coffee was in the back seat, this time without any of his dogs. Marian, who had been dozing against Billy's shoulder, sat up and looked at the vacant street with a detached curiosity. It seemed strange to see the street so empty and silent, where last they had seen it full of knotted groups of men. No stealthy movement in doorways this time, no eyes covertly watching them from under ten-gallon hats—nothing but clean horizontal sunlight on quiet dust, as if nothing lived in this place at all. Marian said, "You still don't want to tell me what you're going to do?"

"It isn't that I don't want to tell you. It's just that it's—it's got to come to you in another way."

"This is a dramatic thing—rather a terrible thing," Marian said, "this coming to the end of a killer's trail."

"Don't look at it that way. I want you to think of this thing with all the impartiality you can. You know now

188

that our western code is a different code. Not the six-gun code of the old days, nor the wild kind of thing some people have tried to make out it is, such as never existed here or any place else. But just a kind of a way of going about things that is bred into dry country men—the way of each man making his own right and wrong, each man looking only to himself for approval in the end. Maybe—you're only going to learn the story of a kind of—a kind of private execution; maybe by a man who believed with all his heart that he was in the right."

She looked at him wonderingly for a minute; she had never heard him talk in that way before. "Billy, Billy, don't you trust me to face out anything, even yet? Don't you think I have any courage at all?"

"I trust your courage more than I've ever trusted anything in my life. Or you wouldn't be here now."

Wheeler drove through the town and turned up a side street to the house where Sheriff Walt Amos lived. Leaving Marian and Old Man Coffee in the car he walked around the little house to the back door; there was a smell of breakfast cooking here, and Walt Amos himself was splashing water over his face and hair at a wash bench beside a pump. The young sheriff straightened up and stared at Wheeler for a long moment through dripping water. "Hardly expected to see you here."

"I've come to make a deal with you," Wheeler said.

"Don't hardly seem there's any deal to be made between you and me. Horse Dunn isn't going out on bail. Get it out of your head." Amos began to dry his face and hair.

"This is something else," Wheeler said. "You've wanted me out of this picture. You've wanted me out of it from the start. You know why, and there's no need for

189

us to go into why."

"I got enough troubles on this range," Amos said, "without outside capital pitching in to make things worse for the common run of cowmen."

"In short, you and your gang has been afraid I'd help Dunn save the 94. You tried to railroad me, here in Judge Shafer's court—but you didn't get away with it. Maybe you've got other things in mind to try, to get me out of the way of your plans. I don't know anything about that."

"People from outside, that figure to throw in against the best interests of this range—"Amos began.

"All right. Now you've got a chance to get rid of me. You give me what I want and I'll promise you I'll be out of this killing case within twenty-four hours."

"You haven't got any official standing in this case to begin with," Amos pointed out.

"You'd like to see me drag my freight, just the same! And here's how you can get it done."

"Well?"

"Old Man Coffee and Horse Dunn's niece are here with me. Give us an hour to talk to Horse Dunn alone. That's the proposition and all of the proposition."

"And if I do that you'll pull right out of here?"

"Within twenty-four hours. I'll stay out until the killing case against Horse Dunn is cleared up, one way or another. After that maybe I'll come back to the 94 and maybe I'll help it with its finance; I don't say one way or the other. But if you want me out of it for the time being, here's your chance."

"There's a hook in this some place," Amos said. "But I'll take a chance. Horse Dunn's in the jail, where he belongs. I'll take you there and I'll give you an hour."

"Is Gil Baker in jail with him?"

190

"I wouldn't keep a man in jail with a leg busted by gunshot. Wouldn't be any sense to it."

"Glad you've got *some* decent views."

"Thanks."

The Inspiration jail was tiny, but it was perhaps the most modern thing in the town. It sat by itself on a rise of ground two hundred yards behind Walt Amos' house, which was the nearest dwelling. In structure it was a twenty-foot square cube of concrete, with tiny air holes near the roof, and an iron door. Within was an inner cage of steel bars, separated from the outer shell, all the way around, by a corridor four feet wide. The place had no great capacity, but it would have been a double job for a good cracksman to make his way out.

Old Man Coffee was reluctant to visit Horse Dunn here. "Don't hardly seem fitting."

"There's a special reason I want you to come, for a minute or two."

"Have it your own way."

Sheriff Walt Amos swung wide the outer door. "I'm putting you on your honor not to try any funny business," he said. "But in case of doubt—just remember how easy it would be to cut loose on you from the house!"

"You talk like a child," said Coffee.

They filed into the dark chill of the chamber within the concrete, and the door swung behind them, shutting out the sun; but there was no click of the lock.

It seemed strange, Billy Wheeler thought, that the old king of cattle, the man who could not only dream a cow kingdom but make it live, was to be found standing here in a two-by-four jail. Yet, within the black shadows of concrete and steel Horse Dunn towered bigger than ever, straighter than ever; he seemed, not an old man at

191

the end of his rope, but a young giant, easy in his strength. The great sense of latent power that radiated from Horse Dunn made it seem that he only waited here within these cramped walls because he willfully used his own great body as a pawn, laid in hazard while he awaited his advantage.

But there were tears in Marian's eyes. "This is a perfectly wretched, shameful thing!"

Horse Dunn grinned upward and about him at the steel and concrete. The walls could not shame him—it was he who shamed the walls. "A thousand miles of range have to be held by money and cows and men—not by a little tin contrivance palmed off on the county by some hardware salesman. You think they can hold me here an hour, once I decide to move out?"

No one answered him. There where the daylight could hardly enter, the silence had a way of descending sharply, like the closing of iron doors. After a little of that quiet no one could forget that a man had been found dead in the Red Sleep, and another at Ace Springs, and still another at the head of a gorge without a name. Wheeler knew that Old Man Coffee's eyes were watching him, waiting for him to speak. He drew a deep breath and broke the silence.

"Horse," he said, "the whole works has been—kind of stood on its head, since I saw you last."

Horse Dunn's voice rumbled. "Well, that's good!"

Wheeler's voice was very low; he found that he could hardly speak. "No, Horse; it isn't good. This is maybe the worst thing that any of us have come to, ever, in all our long trails."

Held in that sharp, hard silence that could clamp down so suddenly here they could feel the chill of the walls. Wheeler was seeking a way to go on.

Marian was holding her uncle's hand against her cheek, and now Horse drew his hand away. "Billy," he said; and hesitated. Then, "Speak-out, man!" he said at last.

"Two-three different things have happened," Wheeler said. "Marian and I found Lon Magoon dead, a little way back in the hills. Coffee, here, he went to Pahranagat—"

"How'd Magoon die?" Horse Dunn asked.

Wheeler would not be turned aside. "I guess that don't so much matter, Horse, in view of a couple of other things. For one thing, Marian had her horse shot out from under her, in plain light, back in the hills. I've been thinking a whole lot, Horse," he went on, "about how anybody would ever come to take a shot at her. Now—I think I know."

His wits were failing him, there in the clammy dark of the cell. He would have given anything he had to turn back now. But he was staking everything on the courage of a girl; even yet, as he faced it, he believed that if anything in the world could be trusted it was the hidden courage of Marian Dunn.

"What are you coming to, boy?" Horse Dunn said.

"Horse," said Billy Wheeler—"Horse—I know who killed Marian's pony last night; and I know why."

He saw Horse Dunn's big shaggy head sway and tip a little to one side as the old man sought to peer more closely into Wheeler's eyes. "If you know that—" he began.

Wheeler's voice was flat and relaxed with utter certainty. "You know I do, Horse."

Billy Wheeler could hear his own blood beating in his ears, like a far-off Indian drum; and this time the silence was a terrible silence, unendurable to them all.

"Coffee," Horse Dunn said in an unnatural voice, "I'll talk to this boy alone."

Perhaps some faint persistent hope that he was wrong had lasted somewhere in Billy Wheeler's mind. But when Horse Dunn told Old Man Coffee to go out, Wheeler knew that he had not been wrong, but that they were at the end.

Old Man Coffee moved quickly, with the smooth, sliding stride of one of his own lion hounds. He was glad to be out of there. For a moment the young sun splashed through the open door with the brilliance of a powder flare-up; then the half-dark closed again as Coffee let the door swing shut behind him. They heard the crunch of his heels in the dirt as he walked off down the side of the hill.

"You go too, Marian," Horse Dunn said softly. "Billy and I want too—"

"You want her to stay here, Horse, I think."

"Stay here?" The old man's voice blurred by a strange and unaccustomed uncertainty. "You want her to stay here?"

"It's you that needs her here," Wheeler told him. Then after a moment he said, almost inaudibly—"Tell her, Horse."

An odd back light from one of the high ventilators outlined Dunn's big shaggy head and the sweep of a great shoulder, but his eyes they could not see. As he spoke it seemed that it was not the big old fighter who stood there, but an old man as vaguely bewildered as a child. "Tell her?" he said dimly. "You want me to tell her—"

Once more the silence descended, brutal, complete; it held on endlessly, as if no one of them was ever going to be able to break it again. And still Horse Dunn did not speak nor move, but stood like a frozen man, a great shadowy figure just beyond the bars. Billy Wheeler tried to say something, anything, to break that terrible taut stillness; but he could not.

Suddenly Marian Dunn stumbled forward against the bars. She reached through, drew Horse Dunn's wrists through the barrier, and hid her face in his two great hands. Her voice came to them choked and smothered.

"I didn't know—I didn't know—"

Horse Dunn's words shuddered as he cried out—"What—what didn't you know?"

"That you—could love me—so much . . ."

CHAPTER TWENTY-SEVEN

WHEELER SAW THE OLD FIGHTER SWAY; BUT IN A moment he was steady again. He spoke across Marian's bent head, and his voice had a hard edge. "You don't know what you're talking about. Old Man Coffee has been loading you with—Look here: is he in on this?"

"I'm virtually certain he knows, though he figured it out different than I did."

"Figured out what? Spit it out, man!"

"Horse," said Wheeler with more sadness in his voice than he had ever known in the world before, "I can name you every step of—"

Horse Dunn's voice blazed up, breaking restraint. *"In God's name, how did you find out?"*

"From something Marian said. After the first shot at her, she said, 'I'm glad it happened. I can't tell you why.' I know now what she meant by that. Those shots proved to her that no one who loved her was mixed up in the Short Crick works. And today it suddenly came to me that just *to fix that idea in her mind* might have been reason enough for dropping those shots near her. Then I remembered the night when you taped up your ankle where it was skinned, and spoke of straightening your spur. Of course, a spur doesn't skin a man's ankle bone. Some boot weapon would have to do that; and a derringer would have fitted in—a derringer carrying a shotgun shell. The shot in the saddle fooled Coffee, for a while; it looked to him like it came from farther away than the horses had stood apart, and made him think there was a third man. But I just happened to think that the shot could have come from a short, weak gun with the same effect. Well—" Wheeler finished— "Coffee has been to Pahranagat; he found out that Flagg came through there like a bum."

"Dear God," Horse Dunn whispered. "It's—the end of the rope." He pulled his hands away, and began to pace the two strides that the cell permitted—back and forth, back and forth.

"Marian," Wheeler begged, "tell him you see—"

Marian raised her face, surprisingly in command of herself again. Her voice was steady. "I do see it! I see it all!"

Dunn's pacing stopped; he raised big shaking hands, pleading hands. "And yet you—you ain't—you don't think—"

Marian cried out to him—and there was pain in her voice, but there was glory in it, too— "I think nobody ever loved anybody so much as you have proved you love me!"

"I—I can't hardly believe—" Horse Dunn sagged down onto the bare steel cot within his cell. "Marian, if you're telling me that you—you know—and yet you're backing me, still—"

196

The girl was pressed against the bars that kept her from him. "I'm telling you that I believe in you with all my heart!"

Horse Dunn stood up slowly, like a man in a dream. The light within the concrete walls had strengthened with the rising of the sun—or perhaps it was only that their eyes had become more accustomed to the half-dark; but now they could see that into Horse Dunn's face had come a war-like glory. Once more he looked like a young man. The girl reached through the bars and upward to grasp his great shaggy head between her hands.

Horse Dunn said, "How much have you told her, boy?"

"She knows only what she's guessed, I think. The rest of the story has to come from you."

The boss of the 94 appeared to consider for what seemed a long time. "I—I don't know as I can make out to do that. Life hasn't gone easy, or smooth, with me. Other times, long ago, I've faced down other men, more men than these. But I swear I never raised gun to any man, without he got his break! I stood with empty hands, always, until their guns showed from the leather."

"She has to know it all," Billy insisted; "from the beginning."

"I can hardly expect her to understand how it come up. Those shots I threw so close to her—that's the crazy part, that a man can't hardly explain. I couldn't ever have done it, if I didn't know for certain that I could put a slug into a two-bit piece at a hundred yards—ten out of ten, easy as you'd put your finger on a nail. It seems a wild and crazy thing, even to me. But—I tell you, never a man lived that could throw the fear into me that

197

this kid has always been able to—just on the scare that she'd quit me. And I thought if there was one thing she'd be sure of on earth, it was that I'd give my life to save the least hair of her head from harm. And I took that way; so that she'd always be dead certain, whatever might happen or be proved later, that it couldn't be true that it was me killed Flagg."

"Oh, Horse, Horse," Marian said, "how did it ever happen?"

"The shoot-out with Flagg, you mean?"

He told them now, step by step; the story of an old gunfighter, and old ideals of justice and right. It came out haltingly, as Horse Dunn paced. But even told slowly, and with an effort greater than they could know, that story was brief.

Until he met Bob Flagg on the Red Sleep trail, Dunn had had no advance word of his partner's arrival. At that time he had already been waiting for Flagg's arrival for weeks—the very existence of the 94 depended upon him; and Dunn was shocked and astonished to meet a frayed-out man on a worthless horse and a saddle borrowed from a rustler—and recognize this man as his Arizona partner.

And then, riding toward the 94 with Flagg, Dunn had learned the truth. There had been no sale of the Flagg-Dunn ranch, and there were no proceeds. There had been no such ranch for more than two years!

Bob Flagg had neither been completely crooked, nor completely foolish; but a combination of some folly and some crookedness had been more than enough to break the brand when the beef market failed. To Dunn, in the moment of discovery, it must have seemed that Marian's property—for the Arizona ranch was to have saved Marian's 94—had been gambled away by his cheating partner.

"There was only one thing to do," Horse Dunn said now with an odd simplicity. "Bob Flagg knew it as well as me. You have to say this for him—he put off facing the music for two years; but in the end he come and faced it like a man. I said to him, 'Bob, I can't let this pass.' He said, 'I know it, Horse.' I said, 'Bob, I aim to turn my back. Fire your first shot into the air. When I hear your gun, I'll turn and draw.' His second shot sung over me, for I had to stoop to go for the only gun I had, which was an old derringer in my boot; and in the next second I let drive—and he was through."

Slowly, then, old Horse Dunn tried to explain to them how it was he had buried Bob Flagg in the Red Sleep. It had seemed the most natural thing in the world that he should make a suitable burial of his partner in some far, open place. He felt no sense of remorse. He had simply set out to lay away his partner—no less his partner because they had split at the end of the trail.

And then the thought of seeing horror in the eyes of his niece, who would not understand—it suddenly had seemed more than he could face. Never before in all his long career had Horse Dunn concealed from the world anything that he had done. Even this time, his worship of this girl prompted him only to a single trick—the trick that had fooled Old Man Coffee in the Short Creek trailing. He was riding a horse from which the shoes has just been pulled, so that it had deep, long hoofs, with nail splits. He simply rode the horse into the water, dismounted, and trimmed the hoofs flat to the sole, with his knife. It had fooled Coffee; it had not fooled old Rock.

Nor had it fooled Cayuse Cayetano. But Horse rested no great weight in the killing at Ace Springs. Cayuse

199

had been a worthless character; Horse already owed him a heavy debt in missing calves, for Cayetano had been a cow thief in his own right. Horse looked at this shoot-out as an execution long overdue. Yet here too he had given his man a better than even break.

As Wheeler and Coffee had suspected, Lon Magoon had been a distant witness. Magoon was another whose punishment for petty rustling Dunn had considered too long delayed. He too had had best break. But before the great old fighter lesser men seemed to go to pieces, losing their fighting mettle so that there could be only one end.

To overtake Magoon, Horse Dunn had muffled the hoofs of his pony with pads cut from a harness collar, and thus had advanced in silence over naked rock. It was only incidental that the trail of the muffled hoofs had been too obscure for Billy Wheeler to see.

That was all the story. One thing, only one, had warped that whole brief history into something mysterious and strange, distorting it, to Dunn's own bewilderment, past all recognition: that was the old fighter's abject humility, his pathetic, unreasoning panic before the disapproval of Marian, his niece. Without that, that first simple shoot-out would have ended where it had occurred, without any hue or cry or storming up of a range. It had been that one effacing of the trail, and thereafter the silence of Horse Dunn, that had changed it all.

"Horse," said Billy Wheeler, "we've got a good case yet! We'll fight this to the last ditch, until they're sick of fighting. They'll never prove—"

"There'll be no fight on that," Horse Dunn said. "All my life I've faced things out. Behind this girl—there ain't ever again going to be a shadow of any dark thing hid."

Marian said, "Horse—Horse—"

At the sound of her voice the old man seemed to crumple and break. He sat down on the bare steel cot within his cell, bent his head, and ran his big hands through his hair.

The tears were running down Marian's cheeks, but suddenly her head went up. "What he says he'll do—he'll do. No one understands that better than I. But there's one other way. There are still cattle, and open country, and space!"

"You mean—"

"The Argentine! If he's spoken of it once, he's spoken of it a dozen times. If he won't keep quiet and let us fight this thing here—at least we can split this place wide open, and start him on his way!"

Horse Dunn stood up slowly, like a man rising to the light. "Why, Marian—why, Marian—"

"We'll take you out of here! We've still got good men, and horses and guns. Coffee knows the old lost trails that none of these others know. Hold yourself ready—tonight, this very night! We're too much for them yet, you hear? We'll come into this town—"

"Tush, child! I don't care what comes out of this now. I couldn't let you get into stuff like that, for me!"

"This isn't for you," she told him. "This is for me, you hear? We'll—"

The door flared open and shut again as Old Man Coffee slid in. "The sheriff's started up the hill. What more you want to say—say quick!"

"Tonight," Marian said. "Now—you can't argue any more." She pulled down his head, and kissed him, as Walt Amos hauled open the door.

Looking back once more, Billy Wheeler saw that

201

there were tears in the old man's eyes. Yet—he thought he had never seen the face of any man so happy, so serene, so secure in what was ahead. For a moment, though, Billy was troubled. As the door closed between them, Wheeler thought that Dunn's eyes were looking at the girl like the eyes of a man seeing her for the last time.

CHAPTER TWENTY-EIGHT

HORSE DUNN WAITED UNTIL HE WAS CERTAIN THAT IT was dark before he began to count the time. From within the concrete walls he could see no part of the sky, and it was hard to judge the time when you could not see even a single star. It was his intention to wait three hours more. He supposed that his people would choose to strike between midnight and dawn, but he dared not take any risk. Their first reconnaissance into the town must find him long on his way—whatever way that was to be. Just as there must no longer be any dark concealments in the background of Marian's life, so it was also impossible that he allow her the memory of her father's brother as a convicted murderer. Even before the steel door had closed, shutting away his last sight of the girl for whom he had labored so long, he had made up his mind what he must do.

With war and violence so close ahead he knew that he should have been hearing the Indian medicine drums in his blood, like an old war pony smelling battle; but, somewhere along the trail, all that seemed to have gone out of him. He felt no suspense. His only concern was that he should not fail in his judgment of his time. Once as he waited a car came roaring into Inspiration and the sound of its exhaust, coming to him muffled where he lay in the dark on his bare steel cot, was indistinguishable from the voice of Billy Wheeler's roadster. He started up, fearful that he had miscalculated, and delayed too long. But nothing happened; and presently he settled back again.

When he judged that most of his allotted time was gone, he sat up on the edge of the cot, and drew the ancient derringer out of his right boot. His hands automatically tested its well oiled action, raising and lowering the hammer without percussion against the shell. He had never liked that weapon; but he had carried it because it was snub-nosed and lightly built, and fitted in his boot where anyone could see that no gun could go. He pulled off his left boot. Laid close around his ankle, and secured there with a wrap of silk handkerchief, he was carrying four buckshot-loaded shells. Fired from the snub-nosed derringer the shot had poor penetration, as Old Man Coffee had observed; but at short range the shells delivered a sufficiently savage blast, as they had well proved. He now took them into his hand; and, when he had pulled his boot on again, he sat weighing them thoughtfully in his great fist, and thinking of things deep in the past.

Presently Horse Dunn grinned to himself and stood up; and one by one he tossed the shells through the iron bars into the dark. He heard them fall and lose themselves in the black alley around his barred cell. After all, he had never expected to see the Argentine.

The fourth shell he held a moment or two, wondering if it ought not to be—his own. If a man came to the last pinch, and saw for certain what was ahead, it was a pity to leave it to the coyotes to finish him up. But in the end he laughed, easy and indifferent, and tossed the fourth shell after the others into the dark.

The one remaining shell was in the gun. He stretched lazily, yawned deeply to the bottom of his great lungs; and fired his last shell against the iron door.

Up the hill from the sheriff's house came the sound of running feet; the sound stopped outside, and the big keys to the steel door clattered at their locks. This was followed by a brief pause and a low-voiced conference; Dunn recognized Link Bender's voice and a spasm of regret shook him for the lost shells; but he put it away. He heard Walt Amos say, "Well, get back a piece then—that's a better idea anyway. But I'm going to see what the hell here!" The key scraped at the third lock.

Horse Dunn stood up, thrusting the hand which held the derringer into the front of his shirt. With his free hand he gripped a bar of his cell high up, and let his knees sag down and his head fall on his chest as the door swung wide.

Walt Amos was in the open door, gun in one hand, lantern in the other. Dunn made his voice strangle in his throat as he gasped—"Amos—in God's name—"

The young sheriff sprang forward, holstering his weapon. "Christ! How in hell—" He fumbled for a key from his belt chattered it at the door of the inner cell. "Who got you? Man, can you speak?" Amos set the lantern down, swung the inner door; and the snub-nosed derringer that could cut men in two was in his stomach, and Dunn's great fist was clamped on the gun butt for which Amos snatched.

"Reach," Dunn said; and the sheriff's hands went up. Horse jerked the sheriff's gun, and tossed it clattering into the shadows. He turned the sheriff, gripped him by the back of the belt, and nosed the empty derringer into his back.

Amos was cursing bitterly, savagely, a continuous stream. "I read in a book you're supposed to smile when you call me them names," Dunn said. "From the amount of 'em you're spilling I take it you're practically giggling. Well, that's good." He kicked the lantern light into a black shatter, and his voice turned savage as he shoved the sheriff ahead of him into the door opening. "Now, you out there—how about letting drive at this door? Before I wake you up with a shot or two under his arm!"

Walt Amos sung out in a ghastly voice, "For God's sake take care yourselves! He's got me cold!"

Outside, three figures moved abruptly in the clear light of the risen moon; Dunn saw and knew Halliday and Caldwell, but had not time to recognize the third, who raced to take cover around the corner of the jail. He supposed this was Link Bender. He heard Halliday swear, and Cam Caldwell called out a sharp order to the third man. Halliday shouted, "Walt, grapple him!" And Caldwell's thick, sardonic voice said from shadows into which he had disappeared, "Grapple him yourself, you God damned fool!"

Horse Dunn sidled along the wall of the jail, weaving the sheriff's lurching and stumbling figure between himself and the general location of Sam Caldwell. Walt Amos called out, "Link, look out! He's coming round the jail!"

"You got guts, kid," Horse Dunn said. He got around the jail, backed over the crest of the hill. He wished that he knew where Link Bender had gone. Of them all, Link Bender was the fox. Just over the crest was the long adobe wall of a storehouse long since ruined. He got his back against the remains of this wall, and here rested, for he had been almost carrying the sheriff with one

205

hand.

For a moment or two then the night was very still. His eyes were searching shadows, trying to spot his enemies. But what came to his mind then was that the breeze from the desert was fresh and sweet, and very precious in his lungs; and the moonlight that betrayed him was very lovely. And he saw again the light of just such a blue-silver moon as this, that had once played curious tricks as it wavered in the pale hair of the woman who had become Marian's mother.

Suddenly Walt Amos twisted like a mountain lion, and his back was strong as the back of a young horse. Horse smashed out overhand with the gun butt in his fist, and Amos went down as if felled by the blow of a silvertip, and lay quiet.

Dunn half turned; and from the end of the adobe wall flame spurted to the roar of a forty-five.

Horse Dunn flattened himself against the adobe, and his knees bent; the old derringer almost slipped from his fingers, but he caught it and held it tight. Slowly he slid down until he was crouched upon one knee. He was waiting, gathering all his strength. He knew then that if some freak of luck gave him one more chance at his enemies, he would not be able to carry through the promise he had made himself in Marian's name. He had fought too hard through a long life to be able to go down without striking out at his enemies now. He waited, saving his strength.

A figure moved along the shadow of the adobe, coming closer, cautiously. That would be Link Bender. The old fighter could no longer judge distances very well. He waited as long as he dared, in his ebbing strength.

Suddenly Horse Dunn rose straight upward on his

heels, hurled the empty derringer in Bender's face, and lunged forward. His big hands groped in thickening darkness for his enemy's gun arm.

A gun was talking, and a second gun, and a third, filling the night with battle uproar. Horse Dunn stood straight up, staggered backward two steps, found the support of the adobe wall; then folded at the knees and went down slowly, his fingers gripping at the adobe bricks.

CHAPTER TWENTY-NINE

THE 94'S SAND-WEATHERED TOURING CAR STOOD lightless in a clamp of creosote bush a hundred paces off the Inspiration road. Val Douglas and Steve Hurley were draped in the front seat, their legs hanging over the doors. Billy Wheeler lay full length on a running board, trying to doze; and though Marian was supposed to be asleep in the back seat, he knew that she was as broad awake as he.

Steve Hurley kept fretting, hungry for action. "Most likely they've got Coffee and Tulare in the cooler! They should have been back an hour ago."

"More like two hours," Val Douglas thought.

"If we was to drift into that town," Steve said, "either we'd meet 'em on the road, or they're needing our help, by God! I think we oughter—"

"We're plenty close now," Wheeler said. "You can see the lights of the town from here—or could before they all went out. If you think I'm going to take Marian into town—into a shooting scrape—forget it. Unless Tulare and Coffee get back with my car, so that she can go on back to the ranch—I stay here. And so does the car stay here."

"Don't you bother about me," Marian spoke. "I'll get along all right."

It was after midnight. Their plans for the crack-out of Horse Dunn were indefinite, because their information was indefinite. First was necessary the seizure of Walt Amos, for it was known that he carried the keys to the Inspiration lock-up; but the trouble was that they did not know how many deputies were camped with Amos, in his house below the jail. If more than one or two were there, they thought that it would be a good idea to create a gunpowder diversion in some other quarter of the town, to draw away a part of the sheriff's force. Tulare had driven Old Man Coffee into Inspiration to make a reconnaissance, and what they feared now was that the hot temper of Tulare had got both scouts in trouble.

"There ain't much left of the night," Steve complained.

"There's other nights."

"Leave one man here with Marian," Steve suggested, "and let's the rest of us go take that town apart! Or anyway, find out what's up."

They finally agreed upon this; but only after it was conceded to Billy Wheeler that they wait a quarter of an hour more.

That last quarter of an hour dragged out like a week; and still no headlights appeared upon the Inspiration road. "It must be time by now," Steve Hurley insisted.

"Five minutes more."

A gleam of lights showed two miles off in the outskirts of the town; a car was coming out of Inspiration at last. So slowly it came that for a time they were convinced that this could not be the driving of Tulare. Even when Billy Wheeler's roadster pulled up opposite them on the road they stayed quiet for a moment, suspicious that the car was no longer driven by their own men. Then Old Man Coffee sung out. "Billy Wheeler?"

"Here!"

"Billy, let me talk to you a minute—alone."

Val Douglas and Steve Hurley had started piling out, but now they looked at each other and reluctantly settled back. Billy Wheeler trotted across to the other car.

Old Man Coffee dropped his voice to a muffled undertone. "It's all over, kid."

"What's the—"

"Horse Dunn has run his own jail break, pretty near four hours ago. It took us a long time to get the full dope. We got it now. He got clear of the jail, all right, with that same derringer in the sheriff's back, and using the sheriff as a shield. But the deputies mowed him down."

"You sure? You sure this isn't one of Bender's tricks—"

"I saw him laid out," Coffee said.

For a moment Wheeler was silent. He was laboring under heavy shock; but already he was wondering what he was going to say to Horse Dunn's niece. "Did he get anybody?" he asked, half unconscious of what he said.

"He couldn't get a man. He made his break with an empty gun. And they found his ammunition lying on the floor inside."

Tulare whispered, fiercely, "We'll get 'em for this— we'll get 'em if it takes—"

"Kind of late for that," Coffee said.

They were silent again, for a long time. And to Billy Wheeler the night turned suddenly empty, as if a great and living force had gone out of it with Old Man

Coffee's words. "I suppose we may as well be getting back to the ranch," Wheeler said at last.

"Who's going to tell Marian?"

"I'm going to tell Marian. I'll take her back in my car."

Coffee and Tulare stepped down, and followed him reluctantly across to Horse Dunn's battered touring car, where the others waited.

For a moment Billy Wheeler stood silent, one foot on the running board. The eyes of Marian and Steve Hurley and Val Douglas were on his face. Steve Hurley spun the starter and the engine began to purr; he sat waiting to jump the car down the road to Inspiration at the first word.

"Well?" Val Douglas demanded at last.

"No action tonight," Wheeler heard himself tell them. "We'll be going back to the ranch. Marian—you'd better come with me."

"What the—" Steve began.

"Coffee will give you the dope on your way back. We got to get out of here now. Come on, Marian." They stared at him; but presently they obeyed.

Billy Wheeler let the others turn Horse Dunn's car in the road and start back toward the 94, before he started his engine. Even after he had set his roadster rolling he drove slowly, half paralyzed with the dread of what he had to say. He knew that Marian was watching his face, waiting for him to speak.

Suddenly she grasped his arm in both her hands. "Billy—what is it?"

He let his car drift to a long-rolling stop beside the road, and shut off the engine.

"Billy! What's the matter?"

Still he could not speak, but sat with his hands

gripped on the wheel, and his eyes on the far off vanishing tail light of Horse Dunn's car, which Horse would never drive again. Once more he was seeking words, and finding no words at his command.

Then Marian cried out sharply, as if she had read his mind, "It can't be that—Tell me it isn't so!"

"Marian—I can't hardly believe it myself. But—"

"My uncle is—"

"Dead," he said.

Marian Dunn sat perfectly still, so still that he could not hear her breathe. Still he did not look at her, as that incredible silence settled upon them; a silence so complete that somewhere, many yards from where they sat, he presently could hear the faint, small gnawing that a kangaroo rat makes, working to get at the water in a cactus heart.

Over all that vast range the moonlight shone clear and clean as a light radiated by silver; you could even see the distant mountains, and there was a color of deep blue in the dark sky. This was the range that Horse Dunn had won. As far as the eye could reach, all that lean dusty land was under the domination of the 94 brand. Somewhere off in the night, scattered over the miles, were the bunches of cattle which Horse Dunn had branded in Marian's name—scattered and few to the mile, but grazing an area so vast that Horse himself had not known how many they were, within a thousand head. It seemed a strange thing, almost impossible to believe, that the shaggy old fighter who had gained these long miles of desert, built these far-flung herds, would never ride this range again, nor count the scattered beeves, nor see this moonlight, cool and serene and clear, flooding the vast dry land that he loved.

When the silence had grown until he could endure it

211

no more, Billy Wheeler turned his eyes to Marian. She sat as still as a resting kit fox, and her face, turned straight ahead, was as white as the alkali flats under the moon. Only, once, he saw her eyes turn, sweeping the unlimited land that Horse Dunn had fought for in her name.

He tried to say something. "Marian—Marian—"

She turned into his arms, and hid her face in the hollow of his throat. For a few moments her breathing was irregular, but she did not weep. "We—can't let the 94 go under; not—not now."

"It isn't going under," he said. "I tell you, you and I can show this coyote ring such a fight as they've never seen!"

Marian said, "He gave me all his last years, while he was old. He had just one great lasting dream—his dream of a cow kingdom. But somehow I think he could have spent his last years sitting somewhere contentedly in the sun; except that he wanted to do this thing, for me."

"I know."

"Billy, do we have a chance to whip the coyote ring?"

He drew a deep new breath. "We can fight 'em to a standstill, fight 'em till they quit! I can clear the 94 of its debts at a stroke. The next step may be a little different than what he would have done—"

"He'd have wanted you to fight the best way you knew—your own way."

"Then—we can win. Next step is to cut down the uncontrolled herds, and build better herds in their place; make a forty mile fenced pasture of that north land you own—"

"We own," she corrected him.

"—and use the fence forty miles as a barrier, to hold the young heifers clear; get in the best bulls we can buy,

212

by the hundred, at any cost; dig tick dips, and set up chutes; vaccinate all calves against blackleg the day they're branded, dehorn all young stock, make alliances with the feed pen outfits in West Kansas; break through a trail drive to Pahranagat, and ship our own stock, taking the breaks of the market—"

"But the coyote ring?"

"Hire their best men—we'll need a big outfit for the new ways; buy out what little they still own in the Red Rock country—and the coyote ring is done."

"It's a gamble, Billy. If you go into this—it may break you, before you're through."

"We'll go broke together, then! If we can't gamble together—but we will."

"This is what he would have wanted, Billy; I know it is, I know!"

They sat quietly there for a long time, holding each other close. "Billy," Marian whispered, "I have to know one thing more."

"Yes ?"

"How—did he die?"

"He died fighting, Marian; you see—well—"

"You mean he didn't wait for us?"

"That was it. He tried to make it on his own. He still had the derringer. Then it seems—this is an extraordinary thing—he almost made it look as if he had a chance! He held up the sheriff with the derringer in his back, and got out of the jail and broke clear; and died in gunsmoke, weighted down with lead."

"Did he—did he get any of the—"

"That was the strangest thing of all. He had shells for the derringer; but he left them in his cell. He went through it all with an empty gun—yet almost made it clear."

"He did that for me," Marian said in a choked voice. "He knew I hated guns and blood; if it hadn't been for me—"

"It was his own idea; his own way. What he wanted was pretty plain. He knew we would have been drawn in, and mixed up in it forever, if he'd waited for us to get him clear.

So he took the only way out he knew."

"I'm sorry for one thing more than anything else. If only I could have known—could have changed it—"

"Would you have wanted it any different?" he said gently.

"Only this: I'm sorry that his gun was empty, because of me."

After a little while she added, "And one other thing. Before he took his long trail, I wish he had known that you and I have found each other."

"I think he knew. And that was what he wanted too, I think."

"I'm sure he did."

"When the coyote ring is whipped we'll have built him such a monument as few men have had; a monument built of land and cows, and good horses, and men in the saddle."

"The Cattle Kingdom he dreamed, and planned . . ."

They sat silent, close together, their eyes lost in the distances of the range of the 94; and the coyote moon swung low over the Tuscaroras, promising sunrise, the cool soft colors of dawn on the Red Rock, and bacon and coffee cooked by Tia Cara.

THE END

We hope that you enjoyed reading this
Sagebrush Large Print Western.
If you would like to read more Sagebrush titles,
ask your librarian or contact the Publishers:

United States and Canada

Thomas T. Beeler, *Publisher*
Post Office Box 659
Hampton Falls, New Hampshire 038440659
(800) 818-7574

United Kingdom, Eire, and
the Republic of South Africa

Isis Publishing Ltd
7 Centremead
Osney Mead
Oxford OX2 0ES England
(01865) 250333

Australia and New Zealand

Bolinda Publishing Pty. Ltd.
17 Mohr Street
Tullamarine, 3043, Victoria, Australia
(016103) 9338 0666